DEAR AMANDA

Tina reread the letter several times to make sure she wasn't imagining things. *Who is he? And how does he know who I am?* she wondered.

Her heart was pounding in her ears. This was the most exciting, mysterious thing that had ever happened to her. But why would a boy spill his heart out to her, and not reveal his identity?

Whoever he was, Tina realized, she'd already fallen for him. *My secret pen pal . . . but how will I ever figure out who he is?*

Bantam Sweet Dreams Romances
Ask your bookseller for the books you have missed

P.S. I LOVE YOU by Barbara Conklin
LITTLE SISTER by Yvonne Greene
LAURIE'S SONG by Suzanne Rand
PRINCESS AMY by Melinda Pollowitz
CALIFORNIA GIRL by Janet Quin-Harkin
THE POPULARITY PLAN by Rosemary Vernon
GREEN EYES by Suzanne Rand
THE THOROUGHBRED by Joanna Campbell
COVER GIRL by Yvonne Greene
LOVE MATCH by Janet Quin-Harkin
THE PROBLEM WITH LOVE by Rosemary Vernon
NIGHT OF THE PROM by Debra Spector
THE SUMMER JENNY FELL IN LOVE by Barbara Conklin
DANCE OF LOVE by Jocelyn Saal
THINKING OF YOU by Jeanette Nobile
HOW DO YOU SAY GOODBYE by Margaret Burman
ASK ANNIE by Suzanne Rand
TEN-BOY SUMMER by Janet Quin-Harkin
ALL'S FAIR IN LOVE by Jeanne Andrews
SECRET IDENTITY by Joanna Campbell
FALLING IN LOVE AGAIN by Barbara Conklin
THE TROUBLE WITH CHARLIE by Jaye Ellen
HER SECRET SELF by Rhondi Vilott
IT MUST BE MAGIC by Marian Woodruff
TOO YOUNG FOR LOVE by Gailanne Maravel
TRUSTING HEARTS by Jocelyn Saal
NEVER LOVE A COWBOY by Jesse DuKore
LITTLE WHITE LIES by Lois I. Fisher
TOO CLOSE FOR COMFORT by Debra Spector
DAYDREAMER by Janet Quin-Harkin
DEAR AMANDA by Rosemary Vernon
COUNTRY GIRL by Melinda Pollowitz

Dear Amanda

Rosemary Vernon

BANTAM BOOKS
TORONTO • NEW YORK • LONDON • SYDNEY

RL 7, IL age 11 and up

DEAR AMANDA
A Bantam Book / March 1983

Cover photo by Pat Hill

ISBN 0-553-23283-5

Published simultaneously in the United States and Canada

Bantam Books are published by Bantam Books, Inc. Its trademark, consisting of the words "Bantam Books" and the portrayal of a rooster, is Registered in U.S. Patent and Trademark Office and in other countries. Marca Registrada. Bantam Books, Inc., 666 Fifth Avenue, New York, New York 10103.

PRINTED IN THE UNITED STATES OF AMERICA

O 0 9 8 7 6 5 4 3 2 1

Dear Amanda

Chapter One

"Hey, Tina!" Marcy Scofield threaded her way through the packed main hallway of Elton High. It was the first day back, and the corridor looked more like a carnival than a school.

Sixteen-year-old Tina Davis emitted a sigh of relief as she spotted her best friend. Marcy looked really great, her summer tan setting off her blond hair and blue eyes. For the past fifteen minutes, Tina had been surrounded by nervous freshmen who couldn't find or open their lockers and, like a good samaritan, she'd been trying to help every one of them.

"What a madhouse," muttered Marcy. "I'm

glad we're sharing a locker; otherwise, we never would have found each other today."

Around them, boys slapped each other on the back, happy to see one another after the long summer months. Lockers slammed and kids shouted and laughed and waved to their friends, dropping new binders and notebooks. It was noisy, but it was fun to see how people had changed over the summer. Some of the boys looked taller, Tina observed, and more filled out than they had last spring.

Tina's mother would have attributed that sudden growth to the sunshine. She had always thought California children grew taller and stronger because of the mild weather—which really didn't say much for the kids in the rest of the world.

Tina shook her head. She thought less frequently now about the days before her mother had died two years ago—and it was better that way, she knew. Especially now that her father had remarried and the household was taking on a new shape and a slightly new personality. She guessed that was to be expected, since Emily Barton-Davis, her father's new wife, was nothing like Tina's mother had been.

Emily was nice, Tina reflected. Sometimes she'd fix Tina's curly chestnut hair just perfectly, so that it contoured her high cheekbones. And Emily knew just the right colors to suggest in order to highlight Tina's large brown eyes. Emily knew about those things. She also understood how to handle Tina's twin sisters. She'd even gotten them into the habit of setting the dinner table, and they didn't make quite so much of a mess as they used to. But somehow, things weren't quite right between Tina and Emily.

Still, the marriage *had* freed Tina from a lot of responsibilities that had been hers after her mother died. She no longer had to come straight home from school, babysit, fix dinner, and straighten up the house. She even had luxurious hours to do absolutely nothing, if she wanted.

But she didn't enjoy idle time. She was accustomed to keeping busy and wanted to get involved in school activities this year. That was something she'd missed in the last couple of years.

Marcy nudged Tina. "Hey, quit daydreaming and tell me what you're taking." Marcy spread her schedule up against the locker door, smoothing it with the heel of her palm.

"Journalism, geometry, creative writing—"

"Journalism! Ugh!" Marcy eyed her with amazement. "Do you really want to be a reporter? Most of those people are so pushy."

Tina blushed, for Marcy's high-pitched voice had snagged the curiosity of two senior boys—good-looking ones, too. She recognized one as Brandon Wells, a reporter on the Elton *Eagle* staff. For a moment, his blue-green eyes locked with her brown ones, before she looked away.

"Uh, I don't know, Marcy," she explained, grateful that the two boys were now safely out of earshot. "I just wanted to get involved in something. And I like to write." The previous year, Tina's English teacher, Mr. Baum, had recommended her for advanced journalism and had arranged an interview with Ms. Clark, the newspaper adviser.

"Yeah, well, I don't know if journalism's your thing. You've got to be tough, really get out there, like Billie Newman." Marcy adopted a stern expression.

"Like who?" Tina blinked, uncomprehending.

"You know. Billie Newman. On the *L.A. Trib.* On 'Lou Grant' " Marcy nudged her memory.

"Oh, yeah. For a minute there, I had Billie Newman pictured as a five-hundred-pound hulk." Tina giggled.

"Very funny."

The two girls put their heads together to compare schedules. They had been friends since eighth grade, but their interests were totally different. Marcy was mostly taking business courses, while Tina's choices veered toward the arts.

"At least we've got PE and geometry together," Marcy said, folding her schedule into a neat square. "C'mon. Let's go check out the bulletin board."

The bulletin board, located in front of the main office, was covered with first-day-of-school notices: SCIENCE CLUB MEETS TUES., SEPT. 15; COME ONE, COME ALL TO THE TENNIS TRY-OUTS!; STUDENT HONOR SOCIETY MEETING, RM. 15, NEXT WED. 4:00 SHARP.

"You should join that," Marcy said, pointing to the last announcement. "You've been on the honor roll."

"They asked me last year," admitted Tina. "But I was too busy."

A paper airplane glided over Tina's head and hit the honor-meeting notice right on the word *sharp*.

"It's an omen," insisted Marcy. "Now you must join."

Tina didn't answer. Getting used to this new freedom was going to take some time. Here were tons of activities to choose from, and in one way, Tina wanted to try them all, like a greedy child with an open box of chocolates in front of her. But she knew she couldn't handle the whole box. One thing at a time, she cautioned herself, but she made a mental note of the Student Honor Society meeting.

A hesitant tap on the shoulder startled her.

"Could you please tell me where room one-eighteen is?" a wide-eyed, redheaded boy inquired.

Another freshman, mused Tina. "It's down the hall, down the stairs, and to your left. . . ."

Elton High, a solid, imposing stucco building overshadowed by a Spanish tile roof, was, to most newcomers, a pretty confusing school. It had four stories, and the hallways were narrow and old-fashioned, resembling a maze. Like many old buildings, it was sort of quirky, with a long hall leading down to a single storeroom, or a staircase ending in a wall—the crazy result of one of its many renovations.

On Tina's first day, she'd run up that staircase and smacked into the wall. Below her a couple of junior boys had snickered and said,

"There goes another dumb freshman." Her heart had sunk into her shoes. Next, she had stumbled into her math class, only to find out twenty minutes into the class that she had math the following period. She had made an embarrassing exit—with all eyes following her to the door and the sounds of snide comments and laughter ringing in her ears.

Tina's thoughts were interrupted by three boys who, as they barreled down the hallway, managed to bump into not only Tina but two science teachers and a group of kids chatting by their lockers. One of the teachers yelled after them, "No running in the halls," but of course, it was futile.

"Honestly," Tina heard one of the girls in the group say, "some people are so rude." Tina turned to agree. It was Debbie Foster, the head cheerleader. She had been exchanging summer news with a couple of the other cheerleaders and two football players. Debbie gave Tina a big smile. Tina had never talked to Debbie, but she always felt a little awed by her. Debbie was just about the most gorgeous girl in school, with long blond hair and long, shapely legs. But this year, Tina thought, popular people like Debbie *weren't* going to intimidate her.

Turning back to Marcy, Tina said, "Come on, let's not be late for class. It's only the first day."

"Then this is where we part," Marcy grinned. "I'll see you in geometry, OK?"

Marcy scaled the stairs to her business English class, while Tina went straight on to Spanish, composed largely of kids who'd been in her class the year before.

Next was journalism. The classroom was set up differently from other classrooms. It was much larger, accommodating worktables, a few desks, and a "light table," which, Ms. Clark informed newcomers, was for "layouts" and "pasting up." One alcove housed five typewriters, and there was also a darkroom attached to the main room.

Tina had heard that journalism students were afforded the freedom of a press pass, which meant they never had to get hall passes to leave the classrooms like other students. Of course, some kids would abuse the privilege, but it could be valuable when someone wanted to leave a class to get the story of the century.

Looking around the room, Tina noticed a real mix of kids. There were four boys, all jocks, who sought each other out in the first few minutes; two cheerleaders, Nancy Frye and Patti

Arvelas; some student council members; music students; and many others Tina hadn't seen before. How could such a hodgepodge of people put out a paper together? she wondered. But her thoughts were interrupted as Ms. Clark began to talk.

"Some of you have been in this class for years and already know the ropes," she began. Her face was wide and pretty and seemed to light up when she smiled. Tina decided she liked her, right off. "But for you newcomers, this will be a different experience. We put out a four-page paper every three weeks. Each staff member is assigned a story and has one week to complete it. It is your responsibility to see that your work is handed in on time. And please, if you're stuck, don't hesitate to ask for help. Everyone helps each other in this class."

"In case you've never taken a good look at the *Eagle* before—take a look at it now." Ms. Clark passed around copies of the previous year's paper. "The first page is general news, the second is editorial, page three is features, and four is sports. Now during this first week, we'll decide who'll be editor-in-chief, who'll be the page editors, and we'll start working toward our first issue."

Then she introduced the previous year's staff, one of whom was Brandon Wells. He bowed grandly to a burst of applause. Ms. Clark talked about the paper's schedule and then went on to discuss some general ground rules for journalism, such as how long each paragraph should be and what kinds of facts to include. Infected by Ms. Clark's enthusiasm, Tina found herself just itching to begin writing.

She bent over an old copy of the *Eagle*, focusing all her attention on it. She didn't notice Brandon Wells until he was directly in front of her. She looked up to see the buttons of his yellow-striped rugby shirt, and next, his blue-green eyes, on a level with her own. A hot flush came over her—he was so close to her, and he was looking right into her face.

"Hi. You must be new," he said, leaning back against the adviser's desk. Tina was vaguely aware that a few papers crackled beneath his weight, but her senses were mostly occupied by his tanned good looks, gorgeous eyes, and slick smile.

"Uh—yes, I mean—no. New to the paper," she stammered, feeling dumb. She tried to concentrate on a point just above his eyes, where a lock of his light brown hair fell away from the neatly combed part.

He grinned, folding his arms casually across his chest. "So what brings you to journalism?" His question was posed as a sort of challenge, or maybe it was just the way Tina interpreted it. She couldn't be sure.

"Well, I—I like to write," she said. "I guess that's why I'm here."

"Not everyone who likes to write makes a good journalist," he responded knowledgeably, obviously anticipating a reaction.

Tina swallowed hard. "That's interesting," she managed stiffly. "Who does make a good one?"

"We ambitious, organizer types," he replied jokingly.

"Oh, is that so?" Tina was so taken off guard that she couldn't think of anything else to say, though she would have liked to knock him between the eyes with something intelligent. Who did he think he was, anyway? she fumed silently, averting her gaze to the open newspaper so that he wouldn't see her blush. This boy's self-assured air really made her uncomfortable.

Ms. Clark called everyone together around the light table. Brandon winked at Tina and slid past her to stand with members of the last year's staff. Relieved, Tina tried to concentrate on what Ms. Clark was saying and to blot out

Brandon's hearty chuckles at the other end of the room. In one way she was sorry they'd been interrupted, but she was glad to get away from his penetrating gaze.

"I didn't get a chance to tell you this morning," Marcy announced at lunch. "Dallas is trying out for varsity football."

"That's great," Tina said. Dallas Mercer was Marcy's boyfriend, and went to Chester High, across town.

"Only trouble is, if he gets it, I'm out in the cold. I'll never see him," lamented Marcy.

"Sure you will. You don't want to see him all the time, do you? That'd get boring."

"I'll never get bored with Dallas. Never!"

Tina smiled and shrugged. After all, what did she know about boys? She'd only had a couple of dates in her entire life. There were many boys Tina had admired from afar, but she hadn't had much time to date, until now.

"What if you wanted to try out for something like pom-pom girl, and he didn't want you to because he wouldn't get to see you? Wouldn't that cramp your style?" Tina asked.

"Ha. Me, a pom-pom girl? With these bird legs? Be serious!" But then Marcy grew thoughtful. "Yeah, I guess so. I would probably get really upset if I had that kind of chance and he tried to blow it for me. You're right. You really know how to give advice, Tina. I don't know what I'd do without you to help me with my love life."

Tina laughed. "Maybe one of these years, some guy will fall madly in love with me, and then you can give me some advice. But don't hold your breath waiting."

"Oh, come on, Tina," said Marcy encouragingly. "Now that you've got more time to devote to your social life, you'll have lots of dates."

"I'm sure they're just standing in line waiting for their chance," Tina shot back sarcastically.

"Listen to you! You're a super person with a great personality and cute, too. Why wouldn't guys want to date you?"

"We'll see," Tina said. She didn't believe a word of it.

"What are you complaining about, Tina?" Barbara Hopkins slid into the seat next to Tina and Marcy, her curly red hair flying in all directions.

"We're just discussing Tina's prospective love life," said Marcy, winking at Tina.

"Which adds up to zero." Tina smiled for both girls' benefit, listening halfheartedly while they discussed her as if she were a marketable commodity. Ugh.

If she ever fell in love, Tina had decided a long time ago, it wouldn't be planned—it would just happen. As she figured it, you waited for it to happen, you didn't just run out and start trying to create the situation, as her friends were suggesting.

Brandon Wells's blue-green eyes came into her thoughts. She shivered just a bit. *"What brings you to journalism?"* he'd asked her, and then, *"Not everyone who likes to write makes a good journalist."*

Will I? Tina questioned herself, only half hearing the quick chatter of her friends. I'm not the super outgoing type, so why does the school paper appeal to me?

The article that had gained her entry into the journalism class, a story about a local company's dumping of industrial wastes into the San Tomas River, which ran through the town, had been well received by Ms. Clark. But was it enough? She certainly didn't fit Brandon's concept of a newsperson—an "ambitious, organizer" type.

His attitude irked her, but there was something more—Tina was annoyed with herself for going numb in his presence, embarrassed at being taken by his good looks. He probably has that same effect on lots of girls, she guessed. He was so handsome—but he'd challenged her in such a mocking way. And he'd implied that she wouldn't be able to cut it as a newsperson. Tina decided right then and there that it didn't matter what kind of personality she was supposed to have; she was going to do her best on the staff of the *Eagle* this year. She'd show him she had what it took. She'd prove him wrong!

Chapter Two

"How was school?" Tina's stepmother Emily asked, her violet, wide-set eyes searching Tina's for an answer, as though she expected Tina's day to be a real adventure.

"Oh, fine. Busy, like every first day of school." Tina smiled, dropping her books on the kitchen table.

Tina thought Emily had the most beautiful eyes she'd ever seen. They were truly violet—not blue or gray—and fringed with dark lashes. Her short, dark hair was always perfectly in place, the way Tina wished hers would fall.

Tina's mother had been much plainer, with round, plump features and pale, flaxen hair.

This bothered Tina, and it seemed that every day she had to bury a little seed of jealousy when she saw Emily working in the garden, comforting one of the twins, or baking some delicious dessert in her mother's kitchen.

The eight-year-old twins had enfolded Emily easily into their lives, involving her in brownie making, swimming lessons, field trips, and ballet lessons. Sometimes Tina wondered if they'd already forgotten that they once had a real mother. But she knew that wasn't the case. Holly and Heather still occasionally spoke of their real mother, but for little children, memories couldn't comfort their nightmares or bandage their skinned knees. And Emily could do all of those things.

Emily fit in very nicely with the Davis family, a sore point with Tina. She would have preferred her stepmother to have some difficulty adjusting—perhaps she would have been easier to dislike that way. Emily made great efforts to be accepted by the girls, and Tina thought she often bent over backward just to please them. It worked with the twins, but something in Tina resisted. She was certain she could never quite get used to the sight of this beautiful woman in her house.

Tina glanced over at Emily. She even looked

great in an old apron. What could they possibly have in common?

"Have a brownie and tell me about your classes," Emily urged.

Tina should have known—"fine" was not an adequate description of a day for Emily. She wanted all the details.

"Uh, sure." Tina reached for a brownie, and Emily poured her a glass of milk. "I'm taking journalism this year, the only different thing on my schedule. My other classes are all basic. . . ." She rattled them off between bites.

"Journalism, is it? Does that mean you'll be working on the school newspaper?" Emily brought a cup of coffee to the table and sat down across from her.

"Sure does." Tina grinned.

"Your father says you write excellent school reports. You should be good at newspaper writing," Emily offered. "Are there any nice boys in the class?"

Tina shrugged, ignoring the picture of Brandon that sprang quickly to mind. "I don't know yet. I haven't really had a chance to look," she fibbed.

"This will be a great year for you." Emily patted her hand warmly. "You're going to meet somebody special, I'm sure of it."

As if I was deprived of the opportunity before? Tina thought, with slight irritation. But then, Emily was only trying to be nice, she reminded herself, feeling a little guilty for her negative thoughts. To Emily the last couple of years of Tina's childhood must look pretty bleak.

"Sure." Tina rose, washed out her glass, and set it on the drainer. "I've got homework."

At that moment the sliding glass door to the patio whooshed open, and the twins bowled their way into the kitchen, dumping their backpacks on the table in an untidy mound.

They were identical, cornsilk-blond urchins, with pixyish, round faces and the hazel eyes of their mother. For people who had trouble telling them apart, Tina always advised them that Holly had a large mole on the underside of her chin and Heather didn't. Holly was also the one with the louder voice.

"Guess who our teacher is?" Holly piped merrily. "Mr. Towner, and he's really nice."

"Teachers are always nice on the first day of school," Tina said knowingly.

"Oh, I can just tell he's going to be nice forever," Holly insisted, reaching for a brownie. "Mmmm. Good."

"How do you know?" taunted Heather. "He might turn into a monster."

"He won't!"

"He will!"

They continued badgering each other until Emily diverted their attention to milk and more brownies.

Tina had to hand it to Emily. She knew how to calm the twins down, and they could be pretty wild and exasperating at times.

Taking her books out to the patio, Tina settled herself on the wooden swing and laid her papers out on a redwood table. She and her dad had set the bricks themselves; then the twins had helped her plant the moss in the cracks. Now the moss was a moist, green border that had spread out into the lawn, luxurious to bare feet. They had arranged the outdoor furniture—a wrought-iron chair, the wooden swing, and an old whiskey cask turned upside down to serve as a table—in a horseshoe beneath a drooping willow tree, which lent its cool shade in the hot summer months.

Tina riffled through one of the paperbacks she had received in US history. It was fun to have all new books, even if some were second-hand. There was an excitement about a new school year that Tina always felt, no matter what her subjects were going to be. This year seemed particularly exciting.

Tina picked the newspaper off the grass beside her. Emily must have been reading it, Tina thought. Like most small-town newspapers, the *Herald* did not carry much news, just a rehash of state and worldwide items and the local news of the day.

Tina took particular notice of the headlines, how the stories were put together, and what types of stories were most interesting, since Ms. Clark had asked everyone to think about what they would like to see in this year's *Eagle.*

The writing was straightforward, and the most important facts were set down first, just like Ms. Clark had explained. One of Ms. Clark's former students, Harry Wendell, had gone on to work for the *Herald* and wrote a car column, "Wendell on Wheels." Tina looked through the issue and located good old Wendell.

She skimmed through features, wedding announcements, and as she had done for as long as she could remember, she read the Ann Landers column. A husband complained about his wife's handmade sweaters, a teenaged girl wanted advice about her love life, and a woman griped about her noisy neighbors. In every case, Ann Landers replied with humor and compassion.

All of a sudden Tina had a brainstorm. She looked through a few old copies of the *Eagle* that she'd taken home with her. Not a single advice column! There was "Xanadu," the rock news column, and "Tiger Time," a collection of short sports items about the Tigers, Elton's varsity football team, but there was nothing like Ann Landers' column.

Giving advice was what Tina was good at. Her friends said that she listened, that she was a good sounding board—so why couldn't Tina Davis be a sounding board for the entire school?

It would be easier to give advice to anonymous letter writers. You could be more honest, Tina thought, which was difficult when you were face to face with someone you cared a great deal about, like Marcy, for instance. Tina remembered trying to help Marcy when her last boyfriend, Scott Johnson, had broken up with her.

In a similar situation, Tina could write an answer such as, *Though your heart is breaking into a million pieces, it looks to me like you should let this boy go. You can't make him like you when he doesn't. So do what's best for both of you—say goodbye.*

Oh, how wonderful it would look written out! Tina could just see it—a slim little column down one side of maybe page two with her byline.

Tina's thoughts were interrupted by a shriek

from Holly. "Daddy's home!" The twins tumbled outside to greet him, noisily spilling the news of their day.

Tina watched him pick up first one then the other little girl. He was muscular—he'd been on the wrestling team in college—and still liked to keep in shape. But since Emily had been cooking for him, he'd put on a few extra pounds. His face was round and warm. He had a dimple in his chin and the same large brown eyes as Tina.

"So how was your day, Princess?" he inquired of Tina, over the noise of the twins.

The old pet name sometimes made her feel like a little girl. "Oh, fine," she answered, deciding not to tell him about her brainstorm. She wanted to discuss it first with Ms. Clark.

Handing the newspaper to her father, Tina thought, Thanks for the brilliant idea, Ann Landers. This is going to be the best addition to the *Eagle* ever.

Chapter Three

Robbie Biggs was a natural choice for editor-in-chief. He had a mountain of energy, talked a mile a minute, and seemed to have the amazing ability to be in two places at once. Since his sophomore year, he'd been warning everybody he was going to be editor when he became a senior.

Brandon Wells was chosen first-page editor; Jason Horne, page two; Patti Arvelas, page three; and Scott Nelson, one of the jocks, got the coveted page four. Patricia Thomas was chosen advertising manager, and Marty Ross became photo editor.

These decisions and many more were made

at the first journalism meeting. When the bell rang, there was still some disagreement about what columns would run that year.

After class Tina approached Ms. Clark about the advice column.

"I'm glad you came to talk to me about it first." Ms. Clark smiled, smoothing back a wisp of gingery hair. "I think it's a good idea, and we've had such columns in the past. The main problem, however, is that readers take the advice very seriously. Some don't, of course, but many do. And if you aren't careful, your column can get you into trouble.

"I think it might be better if you remained anonymous to your readers, as they do to you," she went on. "We've never done that before, but it's worth a try. Of course, they'll know you're on the staff, and the staff is so nosy it'll be very hard to keep it from them."

Tina nodded excitedly. "I haven't told anyone," she breathed. "I didn't want anyone to laugh at the idea before I even talked to you."

"Ha! Does anyone laugh at Ann Landers? Or her sister, Abby? No—those women are respected. Their readers love them, and yours will love you, too, if you handle them right."

Tina shivered involuntarily. "What do I do first?"

"Well, first, I'll make the announcement that this column is going to run. There will be some moaning and groaning when the staff discovers they won't know who the columnist is, and there will be a lot of curiosity, so keep your cool." Ms. Clark winked at her, then grew thoughtful. "Next, you'll have to have a name. How about 'Dear Amanda'? How does that sound?"

" 'Dear Amanda.' " Tina let the name roll off her tongue before replying. "I like it. That's who I'll be from now on."

A head popped around the door, startling them both.

"Brandon, what's up?" Ms. Clark asked casually.

"Hi, ladies." He greeted them airily. His eyes moved over Tina quickly, then met the adviser's. "I'm off to the school parade. Gotta cover the action. Bimbo's going with me."

"Bimbo?" Tina looked questioningly from Brandon to Ms. Clark.

Brandon laughed. "No, Bimbo is not our pet elephant. He's one of our photographers. Bill Christensen. You know him—real quiet," he said.

Tina knew who he meant, though she'd never

spoken to him. He was a husky guy who always had a camera slung across his chest.

"Cultivating a new reporter, huh?" Brandon said to Ms. Clark. "Hope she's aware of the competition."

Tina's mouth fell open in surprise at his smugness.

"Goodbye, Brandon." Ms. Clark waved, making it obvious she wanted him to leave.

"So long," Brandon called as he ran off.

"Don't pay any attention to him. He's a very talented young man, but I'm afraid he knows it."

Tina nodded. "So I noticed."

"Underneath it all, he's very sweet, even a bit insecure, I think. OK. We'll run an announcement of your upcoming column in the school bulletin to solicit letters from readers. Your first column might be slim, but as it goes along, you'll get more students interested. You'll have to clear all letters and replies with me first before we show them to the rest of the staff. You ought to know what a difficult task you've set for yourself. Most of these columns run only a few months."

"I think this is going to be fun." Tina grinned with enthusiasm.

Ms. Clark rose and shook her hand firmly. "That's the spirit. And I really think you'll be good at this." Then she added, with emphasis, "*Amanda.*"

They both laughed.

Chapter Four

Tina's first assignment was to cover the Student Honor Society meeting on Wednesday afternoon. She was a little nervous as she found a seat among the group.

About fifteen girls and five boys were already there, all people Tina had gone through school with, although she wasn't well acquainted with any of them except for Barbara, her good friend since ninth grade. The two girls sat together in the back of the room, Tina taking notes.

"We're sending around a roll-call list. If you're interested in joining the group, please sign it, OK?" Roseanne Bardoni, the previous year's president, said.

Donna Wright, who sat next to Barbara, leaned across her and whispered, "Are you going to join, Tina? I didn't think you joined anything!"

"Sure I do!" Tina hissed back defensively. "Right now, I'm doing an article for the *Eagle*."

Donna looked surprised. "Oh, wow."

That was one thing about being out of circulation for so long—everybody was surprised when you finally dusted yourself off and decided to brave the public.

"It's good to have you here," Donna added in a let-me-show-you-around voice. "Last year, when you were asked . . ."

"Last year was different," Tina returned curtly, putting an abrupt end to the conversation.

After the meeting Tina still wasn't sure she wanted to join the group. But it was a good club, and she didn't want to back out of an invitation a second time. She'd have to think it over a bit more.

"Why were you so uptight?" Barbara asked once they were outside.

The sun slanted across the building, turning the stucco a deep yellow. Tina shrugged. "I don't know," she admitted. "It bugs me when people bring up how I was last year. I'm not the same as I was last year."

"Donna was only trying to be nice," Barbara insisted. "She probably doesn't want you to turn down the group like you did last—" Barbara stopped, realizing what she was saying. She shot Tina an apologetic look, and Tina giggled.

"It's OK. Funny. It doesn't bother me, coming from my close friends. I must be awfully touchy."

"While we're on the subject of getting into circulation," Barb went on, "I wondered if you'd like to double with Joe and me tonight."

"Who am I going with? Remember one small point—I don't have a boyfriend."

"We'll supply the blind date."

"Ugh. Thanks, but no thanks." Tina put down the idea quickly.

"How do you know you won't like him?" Barb persisted, readjusting a comb in her hair.

"We're probably totally incompatible. He's probably a jock with two left feet and—" Dear Amanda, she thought, how do I get my friends to stop butting into my life?

"There you go again!" Barbara threw up her hands in despair.

"Honest, Barb, I'd like to, but I've got to type up this article tonight." And answer her very first "Amanda" letter. Of course, she didn't really have to do it right away, but she was anxious to get started.

Barbara peeled off her blazer, folded it, and put it over her arm. She had on a new plaid wool skirt and a long-sleeved blouse. "Ugh, I wish I'd had the sense to wear my summer stuff," complained Barb, fanning herself. "Trouble is, I can't wait to wear my new clothes."

September was the hottest month of the year, and instead of wearing new winter clothes, like a lot of the girls did, Tina always opted for her summer things. "I guess I'm just not that interested in clothes, though sometimes Emily wishes I were," responded Tina, easing through the crowd of kids outside the school.

As a little girl, Tina used to straggle home after school with holes in the knees of her pants, tears in her dresses, dirty socks, and a smudged face. It had always been an effort to consider her appearance, and though she usually looked nicely put together now, she often came home looking sort of disheveled. She frequently forgot to bring a comb with her and never remembered lip gloss unless she saw someone else applying it. And makeup? Emily had encouraged her to wear some, but the most Tina ever wore was a touch of mascara when the family went out to dinner, which wasn't very often.

Tina knew a lot of girls whose full-time occupation was trying to attract boys, but she certainly wouldn't ever be one of them. There were plenty of other things to think about—her father had demonstrated that to her most clearly after her mother's death.

For over a year, he didn't date or give a thought to finding someone else to love. He absorbed himself in his work as a research engineer with an aerospace corporation. When Tina asked him about it, he told her he hadn't *planned* to meet her mother, and he wasn't going to *plan* to meet anyone else. "Anyway," he had said, "somebody would have to fit into our lives, Princess, because we're already set. How many people want to slip into that?"

Barb interrupted Tina's thoughts. "Well, you know how much *I* love clothes. And my mother has been giving me a really hard time about all the money I spend on new outfits. I babysit mainly so that I *can* buy clothes. It doesn't seem fair."

"What you've got to do is keep your cool. Explain how you feel but don't get mad. Show your mother that you really are mature about this. She might lay off criticizing how you spend your money."

"Makes sense, as usual, Tina. I'll give it a try," Barbara said as the girls reached the corner where Barbara turned to go to her house. Tina smiled at her friend.

"Bye, hope it all turns out OK."

Tina ran home and raced upstairs to her room to begin her article. She had decorated her bedroom during her "earth-tone" mood, as she tagged it, but was now adding splashes of bright orange and yellow to the original browns. Her father had built the ceiling-high bookshelves, which held a set of encyclopedias and a jumbled assortment of paperbacks and how-to books, plus a few knickknacks.

On her desktop Tina kept books she loved to refer to every once in a while: a volume of poetry by Edna St. Vincent Millay, a book of quotations, and a collection of her mother's recipes and helpful hints, beautifully handwritten.

Settling herself in the rattan desk chair, Tina wrote, *The Student Honor Society opened the school year with their first meeting on Wednesday, September 20.*

Tina got involved in the article, even though it wasn't really the most interesting subject she'd ever written about. But she wanted it to be real good. After all, it was the first thing she'd done for the paper, and in spite of herself, she began wondering what Brandon would think of it. After several rewordings, she was ready to type it up. Eagerly, Tina ripped open the lone "Amanda" letter.

Dear Amanda,

My boyfriend is insanely jealous. Every time I even look sideways at a guy, he goes crazy. I can't help looking at other people, so what am I going to do?

Green-Eyed Monster's Girl

Tina thought about it for a while, then wrote:

Dear Monster's Girl,

Tell Green that he's being unreasonable. You don't treat him that way, why should you put up with it? You can't walk around with your eyes closed—you might bump into something—or someone.

Amanda

"You must be busy," Emily remarked at dinner. "I haven't heard a peep out of you since you got home."

"You've heard peep-peep-peep on the typewriter." Holly giggled, and Heather joined in.

"An item hot off the press?" her father asked.

"Yes. I had to cover the Student Honor Society meeting today," Tina explained, helping herself to some rice.

"Are there any nice boys?" her father teased.

"Oh, Dad, be serious!" she cried out. "Student Honor is a service organization for the school. It was good experience for me to cover, and also, I'm going to join it."

His eyebrows rose. "Really? Aren't you the busy one?"

"I'm getting really busy. I told you." She grinned at him. "This year's going to be different."

He smiled at her warmly, pride sparkling in his eyes.

After the table was cleared, Tina went back to her work. Marcy phoned to ask if she'd like to go out with a group of kids Friday night to the new roller disco place. Tina felt shy about going, but then she reminded herself that this year was going to be different. Didn't she feel different already? "All right," she said, "I'll go, but you've got to help me learn to skate."

"Of course I will, Tina, Dallas and I both," responded Marcy.

Sure, Tina thought. When Marcy was with Dallas, she tended to forget about anything and everything else. This skating date might end up being a disaster.

Chapter Five

"I hardly know how to skate, let alone dance," Tina whispered to Marcy, who was already hanging on to Dallas. He was so tall and husky that it was a wonder to Tina that he didn't get all tangled up on a pair of skates, but he was remarkably well coordinated.

"Oh, you'll do fine, once you get into the swing of it," Marcy said gaily, but Tina got the impression that her friend was so excited about her own good time she couldn't worry too much about Tina's.

A large group of kids from Elton were there—Roseanne Bardoni, Barb, Donna Wright, the captain of the football team, Larry Jenkins, a whole crowd of cheerleaders and pom-pom girls.

Just as she was about to brave the rink, a redheaded boy skidded up behind her, nearly knocking her down.

"Whoa! Sorry, Tina! Didn't mean it, honest. Are you all right?"

Tina frowned, recognizing him as the freshman she'd seen in the hall the first day at school. "Fine, it's OK," she said.

"Why don't you pick on somebody your own size?" grumbled Marcy, loud enough for others to overhear.

Seeing him shrink and turn nearly purple, Tina said, "Hey, it's really all right. What's your name?"

"Kevin Whitlaw. I'm not much of a skater."

"So I noticed. Neither am I."

"Tina Davis? How've you been?"

Tina spun awkwardly around to see Rick Addison, a boy she'd known in grammar school. The last she'd heard, he had moved to the east side of town and was going to Midlands High.

In awe she took in his appearance—tall, with a striking, lean face and honey blond hair—not at all the skinny eighth grader she remembered.

"Oh, hi. I hardly recognized you," Tina remarked, then wished she hadn't said it when she noted Rick's embarrassment. "How've you been?"

"Great. I'm at Elton now—I transferred in September. Didn't you know?"

The two discussed what classes they were taking and how they liked school.

"Do you come here a lot?" he asked.

"No, this is my first time," Tina admitted, averting her eyes from his pale blue ones. "I don't dance or skate very well, but my friends thought I should try."

He laughed and led her out onto the floor. It was a smooth, shiny rink, unlike the old roller palladium downtown, which was rundown and smelled of dirty gym socks. The music blared from big, clear speakers, competing with the roar of skate wheels.

"I'm not much of a performer myself," Rick said. "But I've had a few lessons and learned a couple of things."

Obviously, that was an understatement. He knew what he was doing on wheels—he dipped, twirled, and skated on one foot. Tina rocked to the music, more conscious of keeping her balance than anything.

Rick was very encouraging, and the feel of his hand holding hers made Tina feel warm all over as they skated. Of course, she knew he held her only to keep her from falling flat on her face, but it was still nice.

After a while Rick let go of her hand and started dancing backward, facing her. Just behind him, Tina caught sight of the red-shirted figure of Brandon Wells, gliding easily around the rink with Debbie Foster. Tina picked up a little speed as Rick did a half-turn and sped toward the middle of the rink. Out of the corner of her eye she saw Brandon looking at her, and then, to her dismay, she fell smack on her bottom. Some of the kids she and Marcy had come with started laughing. Tina turned crimson.

"That was graceful," a voice said. "Could you do that again?"

Tina looked up. It was Brandon.

"Easily."

"Why don't you take a few lessons?" he asked, helping her to her feet.

"I'll think about it," Tina said stiffly.

"Are you OK now?" he asked.

The pressure of his palm against her elbow was comforting, but she pulled away. "I'm fine," she said quickly. He smiled and skated on.

Rick roared up behind her again. "Take my hand, Tina, so you don't fall again." She followed him jerkily. "I think you should learn to skate."

"I don't have time." It came out sounding like she had such a fantastic social life she couldn't fit it in.

"Are you too busy to go out sometime?" Rick asked.

"Uh—no—I'm not," she stuttered, stunned by the invitation. She could just hear Amanda saying, *Tina, you've just got to get your act together. Smile. Tell him to call you.*

Her mouth felt like rubber, but she managed a smile, anyway.

"I have to go now, but I'll call you about the middle of the week, OK?"

"That sounds great," Tina said in a small voice that didn't match the excitement she felt. "Talk to you then." Tina watched Rick skating away and thought how nice he was. Good-looking, too.

Not seeing Brandon anywhere, she wondered if he'd left with Debbie Foster. If he had, so what? she asked herself. He was only the most obnoxious guy in the whole school!

Anyway, Tina Davis had a date with Rick Addison—unbelievable! Just wait until Marcy and Barb heard about it!

Chapter Six

"I don't think it's fair that we don't get to know who this 'Dear Amanda' person is. After all, this is a democratic paper," grumbled Robbie Biggs.

Tina bit her lip, trying her hardest to look as blankly innocent as everyone else.

"Amanda is anonymous so that she can give more effective advice," Ms. Clark said. "In the past we've had problems with these types of columns, so we thought we'd try it this way for a while."

"So we have to bind and gag the teacher in order to find out who Amanda is," muttered Patti.

"I don't think it's going to work." Scott Nelson sighed, stretching long legs into the aisle.

"Sounds all right to me," Brandon said.

"Me, too," Tina agreed.

"You've gotta be a maverick—try anything in the newspaper business," he added knowingly.

Tina's fingertips went numb. Furtively, she glanced around the room, to find Marty Ross, the photo editor, staring at her.

To her relief the subject switched abruptly to the missing space on page two. "Anybody got any ideas for a four-hundred-word piece?"

Tina raised her hand. "There's the new roller palladium. I was there the other night. I thought that might make a good article—lots of Elton kids were there."

"I already have it," Brandon announced, shooting her a prize-winning, triumphant smile.

"Already written?" she asked smoothly.

"Might as well be," he returned confidently. "I've got a good lead all figured out, so just let me take it, OK?"

Tina was fuming. How could he expect her to defer to him like that? Was he an insecure person as Ms. Clark believed? "But I've got a few ideas, too, Brandon," she responded.

"Yeah, sure, but I already told Biggs I'd do the

piece," he said, with finality. "Sorry . . . next time."

"Maybe we could have two different perspectives on the same subject, although I don't know how much you can say about a roller rink," suggested Robbie, running his fingers through his hair. "You did a pretty good job on that article about the Honor Society, Tina. We'll give you something more important for next time."

"Yes, it was a nicely done piece," said Brandon, winking at Tina, but she scowled back.

"Don't choke on your compliments," she returned acidly, and he laughed.

Fortunately, Ms. Clark steered the conversation away from the roller rink, and Tina guessed it was settled that Brandon would do the article. Why was he so sarcastic—as though it was beneath him to say something nice?

Tina was furious. If Debbie Foster wrote an article, Brandon would probably fall all over himself with praise. Maybe if I was prettier . . .

Ha ha. Tina could just imagine Amanda's answer to that:

Dear Prettier,

Looks have nothing to do with brains, you silly girl. Hang in there.

Amanda

After class Ms. Clark handed Tina the "Dear Amanda" mail. Pushed by a full steam of anger, Tina carried her precious cargo of letters to her car and stuffed them into a book bag under the seat.

"That Brandon Wells is so conceited I can't stand him!" Tina said angrily, viciously attacking her chicken sandwich.

Marcy and Barb exchanged glances. "Oh, yeah? Well, that's been common knowledge for a long time. So you're just finding out?"

"He's in journalism with me," Tina explained and related the morning's story.

Marcy pulled apart the bread of her sandwich and stared at what was on it. Barb glanced at it and exclaimed, "Yuck! That stuff again—I'm not trading." Marcy's mother was English and made sandwiches with this black smear-on stuff called Bovril.

"I like it," Marcy responded timidly. Her friends made faces while she took a bite.

"Sounds to me like old Brandon Wells has gotten under your skin," Barb observed, eyeing Tina carefully. "You've got to admit, he *is* a hunk."

"And a pain," Tina added, taking a swallow of milk.

"He left the rink with Debbie Foster the other night, after picking you up off the floor," volunteered Marcy, taking another bite of her sandwich. "Mmmm—this is delicious. You guys have no taste."

"Spare us." All of a sudden, Tina wasn't hungry anymore.

"Hey, look, you're ruining Tina's appetite," clowned Barb, looking closely at her friend. "Or maybe there's more to this than meets the eye," she said, wiggling her ears and eyebrows at the same time. Barb was the only person Tina knew who could do that.

"Like what?" Marcy asked.

"Like maybe Brandon Wells, alias the Hunk, also known as the Pain—has some kind of magical hold on our friend Tina." Barb sat back in her chair with obvious satisfaction.

"Fat chance," Tina retorted, annoyed with herself for even mentioning Brandon's name.

Marcy stared in awe at Barb. "Now why didn't *I* think of that?"

Dear Amanda,

I have a problem with my boyfriend. He used to call me every night, and we'd go out every weekend, but now he calls me twice a week (if I'm lucky) and makes excuses not to go out on the weekends and instead goes out with his friends. I feel like he doesn't care anymore. What shall I do?

Brokenhearted

Dear Brokenhearted,

It looks as if your boyfriend needs some space to do other things besides see you. He probably still cares, so just sit on it and see what happens, and don't cling!

Amanda

Dear Amanda,

I hate the clothes my girlfriend wears, but she thinks she looks great, and all her friends like her the way she is. What can I do to make her change?

Clothes Conscious

Dear Clothes Conscious,

Why try to change her? You sound like a real stuffed shirt to me. If you want somebody who dresses differently, get another girl, or settle with the way this one is.

Amanda

Dear Amanda,

I've got a real problem. There's this girl in one of my classes that I like, but I can't talk to her easily—only about school stuff. I'd love to get to know her and ask her out but don't have the nerve—a real first for me. I've never felt so gutless before. Any ideas?

Mystery Boy

Tina was intrigued with the last one. She'd never considered the dilemma from a boy's point of view before and was curious to know who he and she were. How romantic it would be to have a boy in class watching you, dreaming about you!

But what do you do if you're a boy? Tina wondered. How do you ask a girl out and sound casual about it? Do you ask her while you're conjugating verbs in Spanish or while standing over an opened-up lizard on the dissecting table?

And *how* do you ask? Real casual, like Rick—"Can you go out sometime?" Or a definite invitation—"How about a Coke? The football game? The school play?" And in desperation, maybe, "You pick—any or all of the above."

It took Tina quite some time, but finally she thought Amanda had an answer.

Dear Mystery Boy,

Maybe you should ask this girl to a school or social function, where you could talk about other things and still be around people, in case you run out of things to say. Ask her during one of your casual school conversations—while you're watching amoebas under a microscope, maybe.

Amanda

Ms. Clark loved Amanda's answers, which gave Tina a giant ego boost after Brandon's smart remarks the day before. All the staff members crowded around the light table to read the column as it was pasted up.

The task of pasting up the paper wasn't mandatory for the whole class, only for the editors, but anyone could do it to earn extra credit. Tina wanted to be involved in the whole newspaper process—plus, there was no way anybody, especially Brandon, was going to say she didn't work hard enough for the *Eagle*.

"Listen to this guy who doesn't like what his girlfriend wears. I wonder who that could be." Brandon laughed.

"Only the elusive Amanda knows," Marty Ross said in a Boris Karloff imitation. "Pretty soon she'll hold the secrets of the whole school."

"Oh, I don't know about that, Ross," Scott Nelson said. "Just look for the worst-dressed girl in school—somebody who wears ostrich feathers and combat boots with striped knee socks."

Everybody laughed.

"I just love the answers."

"How's she think up this stuff?"

Patti started giggling. "Hey, if a guy asks one of us out in biology, we'll know who it is."

Marty's gaze swept the room on the lookout for a likely face. But Tina maintained her composure beautifully—not showing one iota of the excitement she felt. "I wonder who this Mystery Boy is," she added. This double identity stuff was getting to be fun!

Friday, the paper came out. One of the advantages of being on the newspaper staff was that you got out of class to deliver papers to all the rooms. Tina experienced a sense of pride as she dropped a bound stack inside the door of each classroom.

Barb caught up with her on the way back to

journalism. Her red hair haloed her pert face in wild disarray. "Hey, Tina, are you going to the game with us tonight? It's going to be a good one!"

"Oh, I don't know, Barb. . . ." Tina hesitated. After all, what did she know about football?

"Aw, come on. It'll be fun. And don't tell me you've got a date or something." Barb made a pouty face that Tina couldn't help but giggle at.

"You know me too well, Barb. OK, I surrender. But I've got a surprise for you."

"What?"

"Rick Addison called me last night. We've got a date for Saturday. We're going to a picnic."

Barb squealed, "Oooh, no kidding, Tina!" And with that, she turned a cartwheel right in the middle of the hallway.

"Honest, Barb, you ought to be a cheerleader. You've got so much enthusiasm."

"You really think so?"

"Either that, or you could bottle that energy and sell it."

Barb giggled. "I like the first suggestion better."

"Me, too. And Barbie—" Tina grinned at her friend, who was trying to stuff her wild curls under a thick headband. "I know this is part of your Get-Tina-Out-of-the-House routine, but thanks for asking me."

"Oh, what a humungus nerd you are, Tina." Barb wagged her head in disgust. "What are friends for, anyway?"

Chapter Seven

Wedged between Marcy and Barbara in the bleachers, Tina expected her eardrums to burst from all the racket her friends were making. Elton was playing the Chester High team, and Marcy's boyfriend Dallas was on that team, so Marcy shook the bleachers every time Dallas got the ball, and when he scrambled for a touchdown, both Tina and Barb thought she would fall on her face with excitement. It didn't help that Marcy was cheering for the wrong team, gaining Elton's disapproval by shrieking while her classmates remained silent.

Tina had hoped the girls would fill her in on the game, and they tried, but they were mostly so busy watching the action themselves that Tina had to figure it out for herself.

But learning about football was a part of getting involved in school, she figured. All the other kids at the game seemed at home, like they'd been doing this for years, and Tina was acutely aware of how many things had gone by without her.

The crowd roared; the cheerleaders and pompom girls leaped around in their blue-and-white-striped skirts. Penny Schneider, Nancy Frye, and Patti Arvelas were all brunettes, so that blond Debbie Foster stood out, a golden girl.

Standing in a blaze of spotlight at the field's edge was Bimbo, shooting the game, and by his side, Brandon Wells. Tina forgot about the game and watched Brandon instead as he casually pointed out moves and yelled every once in a while when a player did something fantastic.

At halftime Kevin Whitlaw tromped up the bleachers to where the three girls sat, blocking Tina's view of Brandon.

"Hi, Tina! Like the game?"

Barb stood up next to him. With their red hair, they made a cute couple. "We were just leaving, weren't we?"

Marcy and Tina giggled. "You two look like

the Bobbsey twins. Are you sure you're not related?"

"Never seen him before in my life," Barb muttered.

"Sure you have—you're in my art class." Kevin beamed.

Barb and Marcy groaned simultaneously.

"We were just going to the snack bar," Marcy said. Eager to lose Kevin, she plunged into the crowd.

"See you later," called Tina, following behind.

"I think he's got a crush on you." Marcy grinned. "All you need is to be followed around by some little creep."

"He's just being friendly, that's all," Tina said, defending him.

"Tall on friendliness, short in size," quipped Barbara, handing out Cokes.

"Look who's talking, half-pint." That was a nickname bestowed on Barb by her father when she was small.

Just then someone knocked into Tina, sloshing her Coke all over her jacket.

"There you go, making a mess of yourself," Brandon teased, his grin cockeyed and somehow, inviting comment.

The crowd squashed them so close together,

Tina could feel the warmth of his breath against her flushed cheeks. "Oh, uh, hi," Tina mumbled, feeling embarrassed.

"Hope it doesn't stain," he remarked, handing her a napkin. "Not such a great game, is it?"

"Well," Tina replied, "I wouldn't really know. I haven't seen too much football. Everyone makes such a big deal about it, but it's just like tackle tag or Johnny-on-the-Pony. You know those games you used to play when you were a kid?"

Brandon laughed. "I can see how you'd be confused. I bet your friends are too busy to explain anything to you. Listen, if you come down to the sidelines, I can show you some stuff. But just for a bit. Bimbo and I have to do some serious work."

Tina felt a shiver of excitement. "Come on, Davis, the team's about to come out," said Brandon, grabbing Tina's hand before she could say a word. She felt another shiver.

Tina spent the next ten minutes absorbed in Brandon's lecture. He seemed so sure of himself and what he was saying. Unfortunately, Elton's team didn't give him much to talk about. They barely got control of the ball at all. But

Tina didn't care about that as she joked with Brandon.

"OK, now that you know the ropes," said Brandon teasingly, "do you think you can cover the next game?"

"I don't know," Tina replied mischievously. "Scott Nelson, our newspaper jock, might think I was trying to move in on his territory, and he's on the wrestling team."

Brandon, laughing, missed seeing a pass fumbled by Elton.

"How about more work and less flirting, Wells," Bimbo said.

"OK, Davis, enough distractions," Brandon said, embarrassed. "This is where the fun stops and the real work starts. See you around." And with that, he turned away from Tina.

Ugh! He was so confusing. At first she had felt so at ease with him, and then he'd made her feel like a little tagalong. "Real work"! If he was so busy, why had he invited her down in the first place?

Tina found her way back to Marcy and Barb again. Eddie Marshall, a tall, thin boy in Tina's Spanish class, was sitting near them.

"How do you like the game so far?" he asked as Tina took her seat.

"Oh, fine. Except I don't think I know what's going on. I've never been to a game before." She felt dumb admitting that.

"Yeah?" Gleefully, Eddie wasted no time explaining playing positions and rules; Tina was sure she couldn't absorb them all in one sitting.

She sat politely through his explanation, however, which wasn't nearly as interesting as Brandon's, while Marcy and Barb made funny faces at her.

"Thanks for telling me about it. Next time I come to a game, maybe I'll know what I'm watching." Tina smiled. Marcy mouthed the words, "Fat chance."

Eddie's ears turned bright red. "You're welcome. Hey, uh, do you have a ride home? Maybe I could give you one?"

"Oh, no, thanks," Tina replied quickly. "I'm going home with Barb." Marcy was now madly stomping on her foot.

After Eddie had left, Marcy turned to Tina. "Why didn't you let him take you home? You can ride home with Barb anytime."

"I know, but I didn't plan to go home with him. Maybe I didn't want to." Tina wasn't sure exactly why she didn't want to, only that it didn't feel right—there would be all those miles of conversation to think of on the way home.

Barb and Marcy exchanged looks. "Hopeless case. You know, it's OK to play the field, Tina. You don't have to be madly in love with Eddie to date him." The possibility of being madly in love with Eddie certainly hadn't entered Tina's mind.

The final touchdown and victory went to Chester High, and Marcy jumped out of her seat and whooped. "I've gotta go," she said. "Tina, get a boyfriend who plays, and you'll learn all you can stand about football." After giving that bit of advice, she hurried past sullen Elton fans to wait for a triumphant, sweaty Dallas.

"Seems like we don't see as much of Marce as we used to," Tina said sadly. Their relationship had changed since Marcy had been dating Dallas. Lately, it was Barb she confided in more often.

"Hey, I know it," Barb said, wrapping her arm around Tina's waist. "But we've always got each other."

At noon Rick Addison arrived to pick Tina up. She led him into the kitchen where her dad and Emily were in the middle of figuring out how many feet of lumber they'd need to build new kitchen cabinets. It was weird introducing a boy when your father could only get his head halfway out from under the sink.

"I'm seeing if I can rearrange the plumbing to get a garbage disposal in here." George Davis's voice bore a close resemblance to that of the Janitor-In-A-Drum.

"Oh. Well, pleased to meet you, Mr. Davis," said Rick, not knowing what else to say.

"Where are you off to again?" George feigned forgetfulness. Tina rolled her eyes in embarrassment.

"The telephone company picnic. My mom's an employee," Rick explained.

"Oooh, can we come?" Heather, who had been hiding between the bar stools, popped out in a flurry of giggles.

Tina shot her a ferocious look, which started both of the twins giggling again.

"We're all going out to look at Formica. Now doesn't that sound exciting?" Emily addressed Holly and Heather, who doubled over on the floor groaning.

"Excuse my sisters," Tina apologized, ushering Rick out the door. "They don't have any manners."

Actually, the twins would have enjoyed the

picnic. Tina didn't see many familiar faces, but there was a lot to look at—baseball and soccer games, cake walks, and donkey rides, all taking place at the same time. From booths lined with pink and orange crepe paper rose the combined aromas of barbecued chicken, spareribs, and baked beans. The tables were covered with orange butcher paper with a different design telephone serving as a centerpiece, and one table was devoted to mouth-watering cakes, pies, and other desserts.

"I just know I'm going to waddle out of here after all this food," said Tina.

"Don't worry. We'll just give each other great big pushes, and we ought to be able to roll all the way home." Rick laughed at his own joke. "Hey, I'll introduce you to a few people."

Rick and Tina strolled around the park, stopping to say hello or to help some of the kids onto the swings.

"There are Debbie and Brandon." Rick pointed in the direction of the soft-drink booth. "Let's go say hi."

Debbie and Brandon! Tina's stomach wrenched into a double knot at the sight of the couple—the last people she expected to see here. And the last thing on earth she wanted to do right ıow was say hi to them—but wouldn't it look unny if she didn't?

Much to Tina's dismay, Debbie looked picture-perfect, framed by the pink and orange decor of he booth. Her hair was tied into a ponytail with a bright pink yarn ribbon, which matched ıer pink halter top.

"Isn't it a great picnic?" Debbie said enthusiastically, leaning against Brandon and bending down to readjust the straps of her sandals. "My dad works for the phone company, does yours?" she added, looking at Rick.

"My mom works there," Rick explained. "Have you met Tina Davis?"

Debbie nodded. "I've seen you around." She seemed friendly.

"I know Tina. She's in journalism with me." Brandon grinned. "Going to be a star reporter, too."

Tina shrugged, feeling embarrassed. "I'm just learning the ropes," she said.

"Did you see that new column—what's her name, Amanda? *Who is that,* Brandon? You know everyone on the paper," Debbie asked.

"Nobody knows. Big newspaper secret," Brandon said.

"Oh, but you can tell me," Debbie pleaded.

"Really, no one knows, Debbie," put in Tina. "We're all dying of curiosity."

"I wouldn't write to someone I didn't know," Debbie said thoughtfully.

"It's an experiment, Deb. And all the replies have to be cleared through our adviser," explained Brandon.

"That sounds better."

The touch of Rick's hand startled Tina. "Excuse us. I see my folks over there. We'll catch you later." Tina followed Rick, wishing they had never run into Brandon and Debbie. The way he called her "Deb" like they were really close, the way they got along so well together. . . . And why was she herself so uptight about it? You'd think she . . .

No! Tina squashed the thought. To admit to herself that she found Brandon attractive was to admit that she'd lost all her marbles.

"Debbie Foster was assigned to show me around Elton when I first transferred," Rick was saying. "She's really nice."

"It seems like Brandon and Debbie are pretty tight," Tina said as offhandedly as she could.

He shrugged. "I don't know. They've been hanging around together a lot lately." Rick squeezed her hand.

He was nice, Tina thought. He didn't make her heart race, but dating him was fun. Maybe it *was* a good idea to play the field. She was changing, thought Tina . . . becoming a different person. Correction . . . two different people, counting Amanda.

Chapter Eight

Dear Amanda,

Everything I say comes out wrong when I talk to this girl I like. Our casual school conversations never turn out—I'm used to making a better impression on girls. I'm not generally shy, but this one keeps me at a distance. She breathes fire.

MB

Dear MB,

Tell your Fire Breather to stop with the smokescreen, please—you really like her. Maybe she'll soften up if she knows how you feel. Let me know how you do.

Amanda

Dear Amanda,

My grandmother snoops in my diary, and there are some things I don't want her to know about—nothing bad, just private stuff, if you know what I mean. How can I get her to stop? She's such a bloodhound that she finds it no matter where I hide it. It's now at my girlfriend's house.

Private Property

Dear Private Prop,

Remind Grandma that you respect her privacy; she must respect yours in return. You are entitled to your private thoughts. Also, I wonder if your diary's safe at your girlfriend's???

Amanda

Amanda,

I don't think you're a 'dear' at all! I think you're crazy for telling me to get another girlfriend because mine doesn't dress right, so you know what I did? I told her she looks like a clown, and now she won't speak to me. I love her—but what do I do now?

Clothes Conscious

Dear Clothes,

Why ask me? You don't want my advice, anyway. I wasn't the one who told you to insult your girlfriend. My only advice to you is, make an apology—you're responsible for your own big mouth.

Amanda

Dear Amanda,

My problem is my mom. How do I get her to stop planning my life? She forces me to take ballet and piano when I hate them. She has a dream that I'm going to be some great stage star, and I don't want to be. Help me!

No Shining Star

Dear Star,

Show Mom that you're old enough to make your own decisions—maybe sign up for an activity you're really interested in. It could be Mom wants you to fulfill her own dream, not noticing that you've got your own.

Amanda

Writing this column was a real lesson in human relationships, Tina thought as she checked over her answers. It was a big responsibility to come up with workable advice, especially with these ongoing problems that MB and Clothes Conscious had.

Curiosity found Tina checking out handwriting and trying to match it with people she knew. She couldn't look at someone at school without wondering, what if he/she was Clothes Conscious, or Brokenhearted, or Mystery Boy. Who would go to the trouble of writing to Amanda, anyway?

Pretty soon I'll be writing to Ann Landers for advice on how to give advice, Tina mused. *Dear Ann, I have this high-school advice column, and I haven't had much experience with love myself, so it's kind of hard to tell people what to do. . . .*

"Knock-knock . . . can I come in?" Emily tapped lightly on Tina's door.

"Sure. Come in."

Emily placed a steaming mug of cocoa on Tina's desk. "A little refreshment for the busy reporter," she said, smoothing Tina's burnished curls away from her face. "How're you doing?"

"Great. I really love this class. It's fun—getting involved in school, I mean." Tina smiled.

Squeezing her shoulder, Emily said, "I'm so glad, Tina. It's time you had fun."

"I don't feel deprived, Emily. Please." The words

came out stiffly, almost reproachfully, and Tina wished she hadn't said anything. But why was it Emily could make her feel like some poor orphaned waif, like that girl in *The Secret Garden*?

"I'm sorry," Emily said, but the moment was awkward and she quickly left.

Tina wished she could say or do something to make things easier for the two of them. Maybe Emily was like No Shining Star's mother—wishing a social life for her that didn't exist. Oh, Amanda, I bet you can't solve this problem, can you?

"Hey, Tina! Wait up!"

Tina spun around to find Eddie Marshall lumbering after her, his books heaped at his side and starting to fall.

"Oh, hi, Eddie. How're you doing?" She glanced at his books. "Need help?"

"No, thanks." He blushed.

"I read in the *Eagle* that you were playing varsity basketball." One advantage of the paper—you could keep tabs on everyone and have something to talk about.

Eddie nodded. "You like the *Eagle*?"

"I'm enjoying it. I never thought of myself as a reporter before."

"Gotta meet those deadlines, huh?" Eddie looked down at his scuffed Nikes. "I was wondering if you'd go to the Homecoming Dance with me."

"Oh, when is it?" Tina was stunned—she was being invited to a formal dance!

"Four weeks away—the twenty-ninth."

"Can I tell you in a couple of days?" she asked, wondering if that was polite. "I mean, I'll have to ask my parents."

"Sure."

He said goodbye. Tina floated to her next class in a daze. She'd wanted to blurt out, yes, I'll go—knowing that her father and Emily would be delighted about it, but she wanted to think about it first.

Rick had asked Tina to go skating at the roller palace that night, doubling with Marcy and Dallas. Barb's date, Mike Parrish, would meet them there later. Now the three girls were over at Marcy's getting ready, trying out new makeup and hair styles. Tina told them about Eddie asking her to go to the Homecoming Dance.

"Snatch it up," advised Marcy. "Might be the only offer you get."

"Maybe Rick will ask you. You like him, don't you?" Barb suggested.

"Yes, I do, but . . ." Her words trailed off. "Decisions, decisions," Tina sighed. "Last year was easy compared to this. All I had to worry about was getting to school on time. How do you handle it?"

Marcy piled her pale hair up so that it draped over her eyebrows, then threw back her head dramatically. "Well, *dahling*, with all our invitations we do get awfully swamped. It's eeny meeny miny moe. . . ."

They all laughed.

"Eddie's the first boy to ask me," Tina said, trying to stop laughing. "Isn't it only fair I go with him?"

Marcy and Barb rolled their eyes. "I hear he kisses like a gorilla."

"Who said that?" Tina asked.

"I don't remember." Barb waved the subject away as if it weren't important. "What're you wearing tonight?"

"Jeans, I guess," replied Tina. She watched her friends trying to decide what Marcy should wear. They yanked shirts off the hangers in the giant walk-in closet and matched them with pants, which were strewn all over the two single beds.

It didn't matter too much to Tina what she wore. She had just as much fun in a T-shirt and jeans, even though her friends insisted she was being very boring.

But by the time Rick and Dallas came to pick them up, Marcy looked gorgeous in black pants and a Chinese-red blouse, Barb had on a purple scoop-neck dress, and Tina was wearing a pair of Marcy's designer jeans, wedge heels, and a silky, teal-blue shirt.

"I feel like an imposter," she grumbled to Marcy as they walked out to the car.

"That's how you're supposed to feel," Marcy told her, smiling. "Like a new person."

Tina giggled nervously. Tonight, looking in the mirror, she *had* seen a new person, an uncertain smile being the only hint of the old Tina. When she sat at her desk as Amanda, she felt confident, grown-up, and in control—somebody who knew who she was, the girl with all the answers. But other times, like now, she looked different but was just plain old Tina Davis, wishing she could *be* Amanda.

"Hey, you look different—good different," complimented Rick as Tina got into the front seat of the car.

"Thanks."

"Marcy has jeans just like yours," Dallas noted.

"Shhh, you're not supposed to notice." Marcy

giggled, climbing in the back and burying her face against his shoulder.

"Did you see that column in the *Eagle* where the guy complained about his girl's clothes?" Rick asked. "I wonder who they are."

"I wonder, too," Tina said.

"I also wonder who writes the column," Rick said. "Amanda sure has a sense of humor."

"Yes, she does," Marcy agreed. "Whoever she is, she's pretty good so far. I mean, that's hard to do—advise people, unless you're experienced, like Ann Landers or Abby."

Rick turned to Tina. "Hey, you're on the paper, Tina."

"Uh-huh. A VIP—Very Insignificant Person, though," she explained quickly.

"Any ideas on our mystery columnist?" he asked.

Tina had a hard time keeping a straight face. "No. None of us have any idea," she said, squelching a strong desire to giggle hysterically.

Rick backed the car out of the driveway, and the subject was dropped as everyone's attention turned to skating.

Chapter Nine

"Oh, Tina, your first formal dance!" Emily cried, hugging her stepdaughter.

"What's the big deal?" Holly asked, her mouth full of Cheerios.

"It's only a big deal if you've never been to one before, Holly," Tina said.

"I've never been. So what?" Heather was busy threading her Cheerios onto a prong of her fork.

"When you get older, Heather, you'll want to go with a nice boy." Emily turned to Tina. "Is it the boy you were out with last night, dear?"

"No, someone else. His name is Eddie Marshall." Truthfully, Tina wished Rick had asked her. They'd had such a good time last night. He had taught her how to dance on skates, and by the end of the evening she had begun to get the hang of it. Maybe she could take lessons after all, except with him for a teacher. . . .

After dropping off Marcy and Dallas at Marcy's house, Rick had driven to an overlook with a view of the entire city. Then he'd leaned over and kissed her in a way that made her shiver. She rested her hands lightly on his shoulders, feeling the delicious sensation of his mouth against hers.

"When can we see each other again?" he had asked huskily, taking her hands in his. "Besides school. School doesn't count." He grinned.

"I'll have to check my schedule," she teased. The scent of Brut cologne and the gentle pressure of his hands on hers were a heady combination. Tina could understand why people in love did crazy things—if love was anything like what she was feeling. I like Rick a lot, but I don't *love* him, she said to herself. Surely when she did fall in love she'd know it. People in love didn't feel ordinary. Rick was someone she enjoyed being with, but . . .

"Tina?"

Tina lifted her head to find Emily staring intently at her.

"Do you like this Eddie?"

"Well, sure. He's nice. I wanted to ask you and Dad before I accepted," she mumbled in reply, feeling silly being caught in the middle of a daydream.

"Of course, it's fine with us. But is this the boy you want to go with?" Emily's lovely face had a frown on it.

"Well, I guess so. Who else is going to ask me?" Does she think I can take my pick?

Emily covered Tina's hand with her own. "That's not a good attitude to take. There must be lots of boys who want to take you to the dance. When I was your age . . ."

"When Emily was your age, she was the belle of the ball." Tina's father entered the room, carrying a stack of department store catalogs, which he dumped on the dining table with a resounding thud. "Homecoming queen, weren't you, Em?" He shot her a look filled with pride.

She laughed. "Oh, yes, those were the good old days."

Tina wanted to say, *but I'm not like you—not homecoming queen material.* She thought of her mother, who had never talked much of a school social life. When she was a girl, her mother had lived on a farm where there was always work to be done, so she was busy at home.

"You'll have to have a dress," remarked Emily. "I'll make you one, if you like, or you can buy one."

Emily was an excellent seamstress, like Tina's mother had been. "I don't care. Whichever is easiest for you."

"Tina, have some enthusiasm. This is an *occasion.*"

But Tina didn't feel particularly excited anymore. In fact, she wished she had never mentioned the dance.

However, either Emily wasn't aware of her discomfort, or she decided to ignore it. The next afternoon she bustled Tina downtown, into yardage shops to check patterns and fabrics. They stopped in Macy's to look at ready-made dresses, and Tina was about to tell her stepmother she wanted to go home, when she spotted a formal that took her breath away.

It was deep green with ivory lace bordering the sleeves and neckline. The soft velour caught the light and sent shimmers down the gathered skirt, which brushed Tina's calves when she tried it on.

Emily circled her, scrutinizing the seams. "I could make it better, and it doesn't fit you as tightly as it should," she insisted. "Listen, we'll get the material and make one just like it. It'll be cheaper, too."

Back to the yardage shop they went. They pored over bolts of green velour but didn't find the same shade nor the same pattern. Tina wanted the dress at Macy's, but she didn't want to hurt Emily's feelings. It was important to her stepmother to do something for her, and she didn't want to spoil that.

"This color is fine," Tina said at last, picking out a deeper green.

"That's so dark, Tina—much darker than you wanted. Look, let's just go back to Macy's and buy the dress, shall we? I can take in the waist for you, and I know you'll be happier."

"Really?" Tina couldn't believe it. She reached out and hugged her stepmother hard.

For once, they understood each other perfectly.

The dress hung on the closet door, price tags spiraling from one sleeve. Below it, a pair of matching green suede heels nestled in their tissue-lined box.

"Wow—it's beautiful, Tina!" exclaimed Marcy. "Have you told Eddie you're going?"

"Not yet. I'll tell him tomorrow. . . . I hope he didn't change his mind!"

"He's not going to do that. What's Rick going to say, though? He really likes you, you know."

Tina shrugged at the mention of Rick's name, but her smile gave away more. "He didn't ask me."

"Emily's terrific for taking you shopping like that."

"I know. She wanted to make me something, but I fell in love with this dress, even though it was too big on me. She's fixing it, though."

"So you've finally discovered clothes . . . and boys. Next you'll be telling me you're in love."

"Ha ha."

"What if Rick asks you to the dance?" Marcy's eyes widened at the prospect.

"What if? He won't, Marce. I'm lucky to be going at all."

Chapter Ten

"Do you like it?" Barb pirouetted down the school corridor to show off her new hairdo.

"It's—interesting," Tina replied carefully. The contrast between Barb's mad froth of red curls and this—one-inch-long all over and a funny not-quite-strawberry-blond color—was shocking, to say the least.

"You don't like it," pouted Barb.

"No, I do. It's just going to take some getting used to." Tina tried to placate her, but nothing could console Barb after a morning of bad reactions at school.

"Listen, Barb, I told Eddie Marshall I could go to the dance with him, and he turned nearly crimson and accidentally shut his fingers in his locker. I can't believe boys get as flustered as I do. Eddie would be a lot more fun if he just relaxed a little."

Barb took the stairs two at a time. "Geez, Tina, you'd think you were born yesterday or something. Boys aren't Martians, you know, they are human." Then, seeing her hasty words reflected in her friend's stiff expression, she added, "Hey, look, I'm sorry. I'm not myself this morning—I've been called everything from a punk rocker to a plucked chicken, and Mike isn't speaking to me."

"That's terrible," Tina said.

"Yes, it is. I think I'm going to wear a wig for the next two months. But, Tina, you've got to relax. Loosen up. Don't take everything so seriously."

"Yeah, sure." There was that quirky feeling of not belonging again. Funny how a few words could send your spirits crashing. Am I so out of it, people think I'm some kind of oddball? Tina thought, trudging into journalism.

The first thing she noticed in the room was Brandon hunched over the electric typewriter, his silky hair outlined against the halo of light. He was so absorbed in what he was doing, Tina guessed he wasn't aware of anything else in the room.

Today, she thought, I'm going to take Barb's advice and not take anything too seriously. She wrote a sign on a discarded piece of poster board and sneakily taped it to the back of Brandon's chair. It read: Do Not Disturb—Writer At Work.

Robbie Biggs laughed when he saw the sign. "I want one of those chairs with *editor* printed on the back."

Brandon fixed him with a foggy, uncomprehending gaze, until he noticed Robbie looking at the back of the chair.

"Hey, that's good! I didn't see who did it . . . was it you, Biggs?"

"Wouldn't waste my time," snorted Robbie, turning his back.

"Hey, Davis. You sure it wasn't you?" Brandon stood over her, his breath ruffling the top of her hair. She could feel her curls spring out of place.

"Who, me?" she asked, blinking at him innocently, while her insides bubbled with excitement.

"Who else? I think there's a little devil underneath that angelic exterior," he quipped, his eyes pinned on her.

"Now why would I do a thing like that? I'm not that type of person."

"Oh, yeah?" Amusement played across his face, and he shook a finger at her. "You know, this class brings out the latent craziness in its members." Casually, he peeled the sign off the back of the chair. "This is your scribble, Davis. You're not so normal, after all."

"Depends on your definition of normal," returned Tina.

Ms. Clark interrupted the exchange with the assignments for the next issue. There was a lot of hand-raising and shouting as everybody clamored for the best ones. Tina didn't pay much attention—she was too busy thinking about Brandon. At least now he knew she had a sense of humor. In his eyes she wasn't totally out of it. Of course, her best claim to fame, the unsung one, was good old Amanda.

"I want two people on the county fair," Ms. Clark called out.

Brandon nudged Tina. "Want to cover the fair with me?" he asked.

Is he kidding? "S-sure," Tina stammered.

"Davis and I'll do it," Brandon announced matter-of-factly.

A mixture of groans, boos, and hisses followed.

Ms. Clark smiled. "Davis and Wells have it."

Brandon shot Tina one of his million-dollar, heart-stopping grins. "So we're going to the fair, Davis."

Tina squeezed her hands tightly together to quiet their trembling, and although she smiled brightly, she was unable to believe what had just happened.

Chapter Eleven

If Tina had been blindfolded, she would have known she was at the county fair by the smells alone—hot dogs, cinnamon rolls, dust, straw, livestock, popcorn, and flowers.

"The Happy Horticulturist'll have to come out here." Brandon nodded at the flower pavilion.

"Who?"

"Biggs—he's into flower arranging. One of these days he's going to do a flower story instead of a fishing story."

Tina laughed. Whenever the paper needed a quick filler, someone came up with a fishing story. Fortunately, Robbie had lots of photos of him and his dad on their fishing trawler for illustration.

"We've got to check that out." Tina pointed to a billowing red-and-white-striped tent. "My twin sisters have displays in there."

"Hey, Davis, we're covering this thing for the *Eagle*. This is no family excursion, ya know." Brandon frowned at her. His eyes were aquamarine in the sunlight, almost translucent.

"We need at least a one-liner on what the elementary schools are doing." Tina forged ahead, and he followed reluctantly.

Artwork covered every available space inside the tent. There was an exploding plaster-of-paris volcano done by one whole class. Holly's masterpiece was a splash of fluorescent fingerpaints, while Heather was the creator of a series of demure pastel pictures. Typical of the twins—always trying to bring attention to their differences, Tina reflected.

"Buy you an ice cream?" offered Brandon, as they walked through the quilt display.

"We haven't had lunch yet."

"So what? Who says we have to eat anything special for lunch?" Brandon stepped up to the counter. "Want one or not? The offer expires in sixty seconds."

"Yes . . . please." Tina averted her gaze. One

minute, she felt comfortable jabbering away with him, and the next minute, just when she had it all together, she turned into a stammering idiot.

"Here, I hope you like nuts." Brandon thrust a chocolate-dipped cone under her nose.

"I do . . . only trouble is, they get stuck in my dentures," Tina said, straight-faced.

Brandon laughed as he licked his ice cream cone. "You're crazy, you know that?"

Tina didn't think she was very funny. She wasn't really sure if he was making fun of her or if he was genuinely amused.

They watched a few minutes of a puppet show, then wandered down to the garden exhibits, which were limited this year as a result of medfly infestation.

"What're we supposed to say about apples?" Brandon slumped down on a bale of straw. "I was meant for bigger and better things. Ms. Clark ought to get one of the agricultural students to cover this."

"It's obvious you're not a Future Farmer of America." Tina laughed. "C'mon, let's go look at the animals. Maybe we can get someone to shed some light on the subject."

They never spoke to anyone, however. Instead, Brandon spotted the tractor exhibit and immediately climbed onto one of the tractors. Tina jumped up, too, and then they clambered from one tractor to another, Brandon doing marvelous imitations of brakes squealing and gears shifting. He looked so funny with his hair flopping over his eyes and his face scrunched up à la *Smokey and the Bandit* that Tina burst out laughing.

Leaning on a tire, which was easily as tall as she was, she squinted up at him. "Come on, Burt Reynolds. Slip back into your newspaperman role. We've got work to do."

Grinning, Brandon tapped the tractor controls and took a flying leap to the ground.

They made the rounds of the large and small animal barns. While Tina took some notes, Brandon leaned into the livestock pens and made noises at the inhabitants, drawing the attention of a few onlookers.

Tina nudged him. "What're you doing? People are watching."

"Just making conversation." He smiled at her. "You've got to speak their language."

One young woman shook her head as if she'd just set eyes on a real nut. "We're doing a study on animal behavior," Tina explained in her most serious tone.

The woman's mouth formed a silent *O*. Brandon and Tina scrambled out of the barn, clutching their mouths in an effort to hold back their laughter.

"Did you see that?" Brandon spluttered. "I think she *believed* you!"

"She thought you were crazy!" Tina giggled. "I had to say something—she might've called the little men in white coats."

Brandon smiled, too. "Come on, I'm starved again. Let's have hors d'oeuvres."

Hors d'oeuvres to Brandon were two extra-long hot dogs, potato chips, french fries, and an orange soda. Tina didn't eat much, but she was thoroughly fascinated watching him devour his food.

"You eat like a horse," she said, tossing a wad of hot dog wrapper into the trash can.

"I'm a growing boy. Aren't you going to eat those fries?" He eyed her carton of fries hungrily.

"Here—you can have them," Tina offered. Brandon bent one and placed it above his upper lip like a mustache.

Tina covered her face with her hands, giggling. He must *like* me, she thought, to be having such a good time.

She opened her notebook on her lap and began to write. It was impossible to concentrate with Brandon sitting next to her, acting crazy, their arms touching.

"You write like I do—all around the edges of the paper. We ought to get an environmentalist award for paper saving," he said.

"It seems like a waste to write just on the lines. Look at all that space," she pointed to the wide-ruled page. Their fingers accidentally touched, and Tina hurriedly pulled hers away, hoping he couldn't see how that brief contact affected her.

He read her notes while he ate. Is this the same feeling I have with Rick? Tina asked herself. If she had the two experiences to put side by side, would one be greater than the other? In her heart Tina knew that one would. She knew, just from sitting next to Brandon, that her feelings were very different—but they were dangerous feelings to have. After all, he and she weren't very well matched, and there was Debbie Foster, too. Besides the fact, she reflected glumly, that he didn't seem to care about *her*, except as someone who was fun to sling around a few jokes with. But he *had* asked her to cover the fair with him. Didn't that count for something?

"Hey, there's Bimbo." Brandon rose and waved to the photographer, who was lumbering across the grass, too absorbed in looking for the perfect shot to notice them. "Anything we missed, Bimbo'll pick up."

"Or we could end up with photos that don't fit our reporting," reminded Tina, thinking of Bill's penchant for telephone poles and puddles. "You know what strange taste he has."

They strolled over to the horse show. "Elton's own Leah Olafson, riding, what's his name . . . Corn Flake?" Brandon scribbled, while Leah gave a stunning performance of dressage on her palomino.

As Leah cantered through the exit, Debbie Foster rode into the ring, her long hair grazing the tooled cowboy belt at her waist. Brandon grinned. "There's Debbie. You know, I've known her since grammar school."

"Oh, really? Is she your girlfriend?" Tina tried asking casually, but resentment wove itself into her words, which she prayed Brandon didn't notice. But it left her vulnerable, as if her heart lay beating outside her body, ready to be stomped on.

He shot her a puzzled look. "Naw. We're just good friends."

Tina felt her face grow bright red. Darn him—he could really get to her—no matter how hard she tried to keep her cool! She was certain he wasn't telling the truth about Debbie.

Meanwhile, Debbie urged her mount into a trot, tipping her hat to the crowd as she left the ring. A born performer, Tina realized dispiritedly, as the crowd responded with a loud burst of applause. How could any guy not be crazy about Debbie?

Brandon smirked at her. "How about Rick Addison, Davis?"

"R-Rick?" she stammered, caught completely off guard.

"Or am I being nosy?" Brandon rose, tucking his pen in his notebook.

"Something like that," Tina shot back, following him up the bleachers. She wished she had something brilliant to say.

"If you say so." Brandon grinned at her from the top step.

What is it with him? Tina wondered. Does he really notice how I spend my time? Or am I dreaming? Or is he just being the pain he always is?

Chapter Twelve

"Hey, Tina . . . thought you might be interested . . . fast-breaking news story in the science building." Eddie Marshall tried to make his voice sound like that of a news anchorman. "Something about dangerous chemicals, I think."

"Wow!" Tina practically hurled her books into her locker and slammed the door. "Thanks, Eddie. You're a doll," she breathed and ran down the hall and across the quad to the science building.

This could be big time, she thought, arriving breathless at the area. Firemen in face masks were carrying old, crusty bottles from the storeroom.

"What's going on?" she asked Ms. Leachman, the geology teacher.

"Mr. Garrett discovered a faint smell in the storage room this morning, so he called the fire department. We're not sure what it is yet."

Tina remembered an article in the *Herald* a few nights before about an explosion out at the junior college during the night. It seemed that some old, forgotten chemical had grown unstable and blown up part of the lab. The explosion had triggered a scare hunt for such chemicals in other school science buildings, where substances no longer in use were often pushed to the back of the cupboard, forgotten, but insidiously dangerous.

The school fire alarm sounded. Students began filing out of the main building into the parking lot. Tina caught sight of Bimbo shooting pictures of the firemen and started toward him.

"Clear the way! No unauthorized people in the area, please," Mr. Redland, the principal, told Tina. She flashed him her press pass. "All right, out on the lawn, then. Don't risk your life, or you might not be here to tell your story," he warned dramatically.

"I think he watches too many police dramas," mumbled Bimbo, kneeling to get a shot of the science building.

Tina found Mr. Garrett next to a fire truck. He was a tall, balding man with a smooth, babyish face. He was already talking to a few firemen. "When I got to school this morning, I noticed the smell. You know we science teachers have noses like bloodhounds." He chuckled. "It was a rotten egg smell, like that of hydrogen sulfide gas. Now if this was a cooking class, I wouldn't have given it a second thought. . . ."

Tina scribbled down everything he said, growing more excited by the minute. She was just about to ask some questions when Mr. Redland pulled him away.

"Beat you to the big story, Davis . . . sorry about that."

At the sound of Brandon's voice, Tina's spirits flip-flopped. She turned to face him.

"The early bird catches the worm," he said, a teasing glint in his eye.

"Not necessarily," she said, keeping her voice cool. "You're not the only one who can write this story, and anyway, who's to say you got here first?"

"Hey, look, I was just kidding," his voice softened. "Sure, we can both write the story, but I've already talked to all these guys, and I know what's going on." He motioned to the team of firemen who were carefully loading airtight containers onto one of the trucks. Then, seeing Tina's expression darken, he added, "I'm sorry for the way I sounded. I guess I got carried away with enthusiasm."

"You make it sound like you've got a monopoly on news, Mr. First-Page Editor," Tina returned hotly.

"Yeah, I can see where you might think that." Brandon shrugged, looking apologetic.

Was he kidding her again? Tina wondered, scrutinizing his back, as he strode over to Mr. Garrett to ask questions. He's making a game out of this. He just wants to make sure he gets a better story than I do . . . what a creep!

What made her so frustrated was that she couldn't decide what type of person Brandon was—the fun, special guy she'd spent a day at the fair with, or the person she met that first day in journalism, the arrogant one. Tina simply couldn't figure him out. Or her feelings for him.

Putting those thoughts aside, Tina hung around to talk to some of the firemen.

"By the odor we figure it might be hydrogen sulfide gas leaking out of their containers, but we can't be sure until we check it out. Anyway, we can't take a chance, so we have to round up every container."

"All it takes for some substances to blow is oxygen, which is kind of scary."

"Or movement . . . what if we had an earthquake?"

Tina hadn't taken chemistry yet, so all of these possibilities never occurred to her. She shivered. "You're awfully brave."

"Somebody's got to do it," one of the men said jovially.

"Hey, over here . . . this young lady is a reporter for her school paper!" A young, brawny-looking man pointed to Tina and waved to another man carrying a TV camera.

"Who, me?" Tina gasped, watching, horrified as the TV cameraman strode toward her with his entourage.

"We'd like you to say a few words on behalf of your school, and you can watch it with your family on the six o'clock news. Channel Eight, OK?" The young man's face broke into an enthusiastic smile.

"But—" Why didn't they pick someone else? Hardly anyone knew who she was at Elton. A nobody! Tina glanced down at her clothes. What a time to start worrying about her appearance! She had on a maroon T-shirt she wore on I-don't-have-anything-else-to-wear days, jeans, and a hooded pink sweater.

Just then the cameraman patted her shoulder. "You look just *fine*. Now tell us something about yourself."

I knew I should've washed my hair last night, Tina thought, her hands starting to sweat at the sight of the microphone in front of her mouth. Well, here goes nothing. . . . "My name is Tina Davis, and I go to Elton High School. I'm also a reporter for the *Eagle*, our school newspaper."

The cameraman smiled into his lens, and the young man with the microphone nodded encouragingly. "Did you have any idea these chemicals were in your school, Tina?"

"No. No one did. Mr. Garrett, one of the chemistry teachers, recognized the smell when he came to school this morning and called the fire department. If it hadn't been for his quick thinking . . ."

"Are you aware that other schools have had this problem—namely Edison Junior College, which had an explosion last week?"

"I read about it in the paper, but you know how you figure it always happens somewhere else, not on your own campus." Tina shoved her sweaty palms into the pockets of her sweater.

"How do you feel about this happening at

your school?" The man made a motion with his hand for Tina to amplify her voice.

"Well, I feel kind of nervous that Elton was in danger without anyone knowing about it. I mean, what other potential dangers might exist around schools that we're not aware of? It might be a good idea for teachers to take stock of their departments on a regular basis. And maybe the students could form a committee to help—"

"Do you feel teachers were at fault here?" the man interrupted.

Tina could feel beads of sweat forming on her brow. She hoped the TV camera didn't pick them up. "Oh, no," she replied quickly. "I'm sure this wasn't anybody's fault. I'm just saying that now that we're aware of the possible dangers, maybe we can form some kind of program. At least make people aware of the dangers. Then we can all keep our eyes—and noses—open."

The commentator looked very pleased. "That *does* sound like a good idea, Tina, and I'd like to see your school do just that."

Wolf whistles and applause erupted around Tina's ears. Half the school had heard her! *Dad isn't going to believe this,* she thought, as kids crowded around her.

"Can I shake your hand, Tina?" Kevin Whitlaw grinned at Tina in adoration. "You were really super!" He reached for her limp hand and pumped it vigorously, while the crowd shouted in delight.

"Yea, Tina! Yea, Elton!" the kids shouted.

If the scene at Elton had been unbelievable, seeing her own face in living color on her own TV set easily topped it. The self-confident girl on the news seemed like a stranger to Tina, especially because she knew how nervous she'd been at the time. She sounded intelligent, and she even looked good!

"Fantastic!" Tina's father said, giving her a bear hug when the telecast ended. "My Tina on TV . . . for an important cause, no less!"

"Daddy, it just *happened*," Tina said. "I was in the right place at the right time."

"Just a lucky break, huh? I don't believe that. You were very mature on TV. You said all the right things. I bet your teachers are going to be really proud of you."

"Let's celebrate," Emily suggested. "I made a banana cake today."

"Now I've got something to talk about for current events tomorrow," Holly remarked.

"No, I'm gonna do it," Heather argued.

They bickered noisily for a few minutes, until

the phone rang and their father finally got them to hush. Tina answered it.

"I saw you on television, Tina," Ms. Clark said proudly. "Aren't you a celebrity? I must say you did very well. Where'd you get that great idea for a safety program? I guess you're doing the article on this?"

"Yes, but—"

"Well, we'll have to get someone to do an article on your TV speech, now won't we?"

Tina's heart rose with Ms. Clark's excitement. Then she realized the importance of Ms. Clark's words. *She* would get the article, not Brandon, because she had been on television. Of course, she wanted to do the story, but now she regretted her argument with Brandon, even though she was still angry with him. But hadn't she promised herself at the beginning of the school year to do her best on the *Eagle*? And no one—especially not Brandon Wells—was going to stand in her way.

The phone rang all evening: Eddie called, and Tina thanked him again for his golden news tip; Marcy and Barb called and were almost more excited than Tina herself; and Rick called, and was also enthusiastic.

Then Brandon called. "Congratulations on

your debut as a TV reporter—or starlet," he said.

Butterflies leaped in Tina's stomach at the sound of his voice. "Thank you—or are you being sarcastic again, Wells?"

"Come on, Davis, I just wanted to congratulate you. You made a great speech."

"I never know when to take you seriously."

He chuckled. "Good," he said and hung up.

Tina stared at the receiver until she heard a dial tone. Brandon was totally unbelievable. Was he serious? Would he call her up if he wasn't?

Tina didn't have time to ponder this as the phone rang again. Everybody wanted to talk to her. Finally, she escaped to her room with a refusal to talk to anyone else. She had to work on "Dear Amanda." As she had told Marcy earlier, being famous didn't mean you could shuck your day-to-day responsibilities.

Dear Amanda,

I was Brokenhearted, but now I'm just plain miserable. You said my boyfriend still cared, but he didn't. He dumped me. A lot you know.

Brokenhearted Turned Miserable

Dear BTM,

I told you he probably still cared, but remember, I don't know either of you. All I can say is, get busy, date, and do things. Time heals all wounds.

Amanda

Tina could certainly attest to her advice here. Time had soothed her own wounds after her mother had died, although often memories could bring back the sense of loss. Even if the death of a parent wasn't the same as losing a boyfriend, dating and being busy helped in both instances. Tina wished she'd pushed herself to do it sooner.

Dear Amanda,

My boyfriend is a male chauvinist pig. When we go on a picnic, he tells me to bring all the food. His whole family is this way. I don't think this is fair.

Standing-Up-For-Rights

Dear Rights,

You're right—he shouldn't expect you to bring the food just because you're a girl. Tell Oink to bring his own sandwich, or better yet, plan the menu so he brings half.

Amanda

Dear Amanda,

My boyfriend wrote to you about my clothes, and boy, was I mad! He doesn't know what style is, Amanda. He's ultraconservative, but I don't criticize his boring taste. Thanks for telling him off. We are now mismatched sweethearts again.

Mismatched

Dear Mismatched,

I'm glad to hear you worked it out. Also, it's nice to know you can love each other without cramping each other's "style"!

Amanda

Dear Amanda,

My mom says you're just a teenager, so what do you know? I guess she's right. I'm writing to Ann Landers now. Maybe Mom will listen to her!

No Shining Star

Dear Amanda,

The girl of my dreams is dating another guy now. She's on top of the world, so it looks like quits for me. I took your advice and asked her out, and everything went fine, I thought. I guess she thought differently. But this doesn't change how I feel about her. I dream about her all the time, and I cut her picture out of last year's yearbook and stuck it on my bulletin board. (No, I'm not going to throw darts at it!) She looks more mature this year, as if things are happening to her and she's happier. Funny, I hardly knew she existed back then . . . but now the tables have turned. So I probably won't be writing to you anymore.

Mystery Boy (and doomed to remain so)

So MB was backing off. The lucky girl wasn't interested, even though they'd had one good time together. He sounded like such a neat guy, too. Maybe the girl didn't realize how lucky she was to be liked by him. Maybe she misinterpreted him. Or maybe, Tina fantasized, he was like Cyrano de Bergerac, who was so madly in love with that beautiful woman and whose every spoken word was fantastic poetry—yet he had this incredibly ugly long nose and hid from her so she wouldn't know what he looked like.

Maybe I'm corresponding with another Cyrano, she thought. But to tell MB what she had to tell herself when it came to Brandon saddened her deeply. Knowing a lost cause when she saw one, Tina realized there was no sense hanging on to a dream. Especially when you and the dream couldn't even get along together. . . .

She felt a slight flutter of hope thinking of Brandon's phone call. But no, she could never be quite sure what Brandon was thinking. . . .

Dear MB,

I'm sorry to hear about you-know-who. I know it's very hard to bear when that someone likes/loves someone else, but if you really care, you'll know when to let go. I think you're probably doing the right thing.

Amanda

Dear Amanda,

I've been going with a guy for a while now, and I've met someone else. I'm not really ready to break up with the first guy, but I really like No. 2, and I can't make up my mind. What do you say?

Double-Trouble

Tina thought the handwriting looked familiar, but she didn't know anyone with that problem.

Dear Trouble,

You'd better sit tight before you make a move. No. 1 isn't going to want to play second fiddle, even if No. 2 is willing. All I can say is, follow your heart—it knows where it wants to go.

Amanda

Follow your heart—what did that mean, exactly? If I followed my heart, where would it lead me? Tina wondered, tantalized by the whole idea of letting her feelings tug her through the twists and turns of her thoughts to whatever lay mysteriously at the end.

Brandon's handsome face filled her mind and before she could stop it, a picture of herself in his arms.

Chapter Thirteen

The next day Marcy ran up to Tina in the hallway as she was walking to journalism.

"Tina, I've got to tell you something!"

"What is it?"

"It's private. Let's find an empty classroom."

"But, Marcy, I'm on my way to a class." Marcy's only answer was to pull Tina into the bathroom. She started to speak abruptly.

"I'm not sure I'm in love with Dallas anymore. I've just met someone else. Aaron Thrasher! Oh, Tina, he's just a dream come true! I don't know what to do!"

"Look, Marcy, just calm down. We'll talk about this at lunchtime. I've got to get to journalism now." Tina added under her breath, "And deal with that pain, Brandon Wells."

"Hey, what is it with you two?" Marcy eyed her friend with curiosity. "If I didn't know you better, I'd swear you had a thing for him."

"It's nothing. Let's talk about it later, Marce, OK?"

Tina left Marcy, feeling a little bad that she hadn't given her friend's problem more attention.

Tina was just nearing the classroom when she felt a tap on her shoulder. It was Rick.

"Can we go out Friday night?" he asked, falling into step beside her.

"Uh, sure. I'd like to." Tina accepted distractedly, concentrating on Marcy's problem and the upcoming confrontation with Brandon.

"I was wondering," Rick persisted, "if you'd like to go to the Homecoming Dance with me." Ahead, Brandon stood inside the classroom door.

"Oh, Rick, I'm sorry, I'd really like to, but I'm already going with someone else. He asked me earlier." Rick smiled weakly and left without even saying goodbye.

He looks so sad, Tina thought, but if he wanted to go to the dance, he should have asked sooner. Still, she was sorry.

When Brandon set eyes on her, Tina melted like a Hershey bar left out in the sun, which really annoyed her because she had carefully pieced together her composure especially for this moment.

As she drew closer, his expression softened into a smile. "You're looking good for someone who's been kept up half the night with congratulatory phone calls," he said, jokingly.

"How'd you know?"

"I'm an old pro, didn't I tell you?" Brandon's grin lit up his whole face. "I've been on TV before. My dad is an ad man, and he used me in a toothpaste commercial once."

Tina giggled. "Well," she said softly, "you know this could've happened to either of us."

"Except that you're prettier than I am." He shot her a sidelong glance, slouching casually against a desk.

Heat climbed up from her collar, filling her cheeks. Was he flattering her or teasing? Or making a mockery out of her success? She couldn't be sure. "You think they picked me because I'm a girl, is that it?"

Brandon held his hands up as if she were pointing a gun at him. "Hey, don't get excited, Tina. I said the wrong thing, sorry. It was supposed to be—a compliment." His grin faded. "I didn't plan on getting into a hassle with you."

"I—I—" Tina stammered, but it was too late.

He was already halfway across the room, and even though part of her wanted to run after him and tell him she was sorry for being overly sensitive, she knew she couldn't risk the whole class knowing what was going on between them.

What is going on between us? Or, what is going on with me? Tina's insides turned to jelly at the blunt knowledge that what Brandon said and did mattered to her so much. She was crazy about him. She'd spent a sleepless night worrying over what would happen today when she saw him, and she thought she had been ready for anything—but she hadn't been ready for him being nice to her. Was there something between the two of them, or was it just that caring about him made every word he said terribly important? And how about the way he looked at her—was there something there?

But whatever he felt, if he felt anything for her at all, it had to be totally squelched by now, Tina knew, because he didn't talk to her or look at her again all period.

"Isn't this Amanda good?" Emily exclaimed. The twins gathered around the open *Eagle* to see what she was talking about. "She's as good as Ann Landers, isn't she, Tina?"

"Almost," Tina replied. Nothing like having

an identity that was a secret even from your parents, she thought.

"Do you know her, Tina?" asked Heather.

"Nobody on the paper knows who she is."

"Maybe she's a boy," Holly speculated, which Heather immediately disagreed with.

In the privacy of her bedroom, Tina drew out a manila envelope, which she recognized as MB's. Here I am, silly Tina Davis, who doesn't know the first thing about solving her own problems, answering the problems of an entire school. Crazy!

At the top of the letter, Tina was surprised to read, PLEASE DON'T PRINT THIS IN THE PAPER!!!!

Dear Amanda,

This might come as a shock to you, but this is one I don't want you to print in the column. Even though you still don't know who I am, I know who you are. You're the girl I've been writing about all this time. In class I'm never able to tell you the way I feel about you, and the places we've been together have not been exactly ideal for declaring love. I still feel we could be good together, if we could get over the bumps.

And I figured out that you're not dating anyone exclusively, but that's really up to you, isn't it?

Always,
Mystery Boy

Tina reread the letter several times to make sure she wasn't imagining things. Who is he? And how does he know who I am? she wondered, turning the envelope inside out in search of a clue. She held the paper up to the light to see if anything had been written on top of the letter so that an imprint might show through, but there was nothing.

Her heart was pounding in her ears. This was the most exciting, mysterious thing that had ever happened to her. But why would a boy spill his heart to her and not reveal his identity? What kind of a nut was he?

Whatever kind of nut he was, Tina realized, she'd already fallen for him. Her secret pen pal . . . who could be Cyrano de Bergerac for all she knew. . . .

He had to be somebody she knew pretty well, she decided, digging out all the "Amanda" letters, which were bound by thick rubber bands. Tina lined up all MB's letters on her desk. The first time, she had advised him to ask the girl to a social event. Just after that Rick took her to the picnic, and Eddie asked her to the Homecoming Dance!

She pulled out a clean sheet of paper and wrote CLUES at the top, then a subheading of SOCIAL EVENT, and the two boys' names below that. One letter said that he was in one of her classes, so she wrote CLASS, and Rick and Eddie's names under it, for PE and geometry respectively. (Briefly, Tina wondered if PE counted since boys and girls didn't mingle.) Maybe whoever it was had caught a glimpse of the letters in her purse. Someone on the *Eagle* staff, maybe?

No, if any member of the staff knew, she or he would tell the whole class. Brandon? Impossible. Brandon was so sure of himself; he'd never write to a girl like that. If he liked someone, he'd just say so, Tina was certain of it. Once Tina had suspected that Marty Ross might have had suspicions that she was Amanda, but they had never dated or anything.

Tina wrote KEEPS ME AT A DISTANCE as another heading. Who did she keep at a distance? Maybe Kevin Whitlaw. Marcy was convinced Kevin had a thing for Tina, and maybe he was intimidated by her because he was an underclassman. He *did* ask her to the basketball tryouts once—did that count as an event? Kevin's name went under SOCIAL EVENT and KEEPS ME AT A DISTANCE.

The girl of my dreams is dating another guy now. . . . That could be Rick, Eddie, or Kevin. *She's on top of the world. . . .* In love, maybe? Was I advertising my excitement about the dance? Tina wondered. Rick might be more disappointed than he let on. And, everywhere she'd been with each of those boys had not been places for "declaring love."

Looking back over her list, she saw that Rick and Kevin's names came up the most. Eddie probably wasn't MB because they were going to the dance together, and he wouldn't have as much reason to feel she didn't like him. Plus, they'd never actually been out together before.

Now to find out—without blowing her cover.

Chapter Fourteen

Tina ran her palms down the front of her new formal.

So much has happened in such a short time, she thought, admiring her image in the full-length mirror. *Mom wouldn't even recognize me now. Me, who never was one to fuss over her appearance, who hardly ever dated. Now I get invited to dances and complimented in letters from an anonymous, exciting boy.*

No doubt, pushing herself into new activities had something to do with the change, although she still felt timid about some things, like being on TV, for instance. And it wasn't all easy, she had lamented to Barb that morning on the phone. Rick pouted all the way through their Friday night date, hardly speaking to her. Which made Tina suspect him as the author of the MB mail even more. But of course, she couldn't tell Barb that.

"I'm not making friends; I'm making enemies, Barb. Rick's mad at me, and all I ever do is fight with Brandon."

"Listen. All's fair in love and war, and newspaper reporting, and homecoming dances." Barb laughed at her own dumb joke.

"I wish I could think so," Tina said.

"Take my word for it. Anyway, if it makes you feel better, Rick'll stop acting like a nerd as soon as he sees it's not getting him anywhere. And from what I know of Wells, he's the oldest in a big family, and he takes on a lot of responsibility. So he thinks he can run the whole world, I guess."

"Oh, yeah?" That interesting little fact about Brandon perked Tina up. Maybe Brandon had a good reason for being the way he was—what had looked obnoxious to her in the beginning. She kept mulling over her conversation with him, trying to make improvements on it, but that didn't help at all since spoken words couldn't be taken back and replaced by ones you wished you'd said.

Tina wondered if he'd be at the dance tonight.

"Tina? Are you ready? Eddie's here." Emily glided through the open doorway, drawing in her breath at the sight of her stepdaughter. "Oh, you look beautiful!"

A lump formed in Tina's throat. "Thank you." Her smile felt all trembly, like she was about to cry. "And thank you for the dress and—"

"Oh, you know you don't have to thank me, Tina," she returned brightly.

"But I do. Thank you for everything you've done for me, Emily. I know you've tried really hard, and I haven't been that great a daughter, and I'm sorry for that. But I want you to know you're really special to me." Tina hugged her tightly, biting back her tears so that they didn't ruin her eye makeup.

"Look, don't be sorry for anything. I never expected it to be easy for any of us." Emily held her at arm's length, her expression tearful but radiant. "If I were you and lost my mother . . . Well, I guess what I'm saying is I try to put myself in your shoes, and I think I understand. Now come on." Emily pressed a soft, sequined purse into Tina's hand. "It's time to go."

"She's coming!" That announcement was followed by munchkin laughter in the hallway.

"All we need now is Bert Parks." Emily giggled, motioning to the twins for quiet.

Eddie was standing in the center of the entry rug, looking handsome in his white dinner jacket and bow tie. "Wow, you look really nice, Tina," he commented, his gaze shifting away from her in embarrassment.

"Thanks, so do you."

"You've probably never seen each other look so nice, have you?" Tina's father chuckled.

"Ugh, Dad." Tina grimaced.

Her father was not to be discouraged, however. Already his tripod was set up to take pictures of the couple, so they were obligated to sit and stand on command through half a roll of film.

"Thank God we're sprung," breathed Eddie once they were outside. "My folks went through the same baloney. They even wanted me to bring you back to the house to take photos. Can you believe it?"

Tina giggled as she tucked her formal carefully beneath her on the car seat. "Yeah, parents will be parents."

"Most of the kids are going to Mario's for Italian food," Eddie said. "I hope that's OK with you?"

Italian food—with her flip-flopping stomach?

"Oh, sure, that sounds wonderful," Tina said, noticing Eddie flush at her words. At least I'm not the only one with the jitters, she thought.

Tina knew that spaghetti was the worst thing in the world to order when out with a date, so she ordered ravioli and watched poor Eddie tangle with the spaghetti. He was nice but shy, and Tina wasn't a great conversationalist herself. She wished they were doubling with somebody so that they didn't have to work so hard just to talk.

Luckily, a few kids came by to compliment Tina on her TV appearance. Larry Jenkins wadded his napkin into the shape of a mike and shoved it under her nose, with, "Got a word for us, Ms. Davis?"

"Yes." Tina grinned at the expectant faces surrounding the table. "What's for dessert?"

Everybody broke up. Eddie looked pleased. "I hope your story turns out as good as those cookies you made me."

Tina laughed. She'd made Eddie chocolate chip cookies as a thank-you for the science scare tip. "Well, if I get an A in journalism, I'll owe it all to you, Eddie."

Eddie turned red. He was saved from answering by Marcy and Dallas, who walked by the table. "Hi, Eddie, hi, Tina. You look super, Tina."

Marcy grinned, but her expression didn't match the mood of the romantic evening, Tina was sorry to see. Dallas, too, looked like he was trying too hard to have a good time.

At the dance Tina found out that Eddie wasn't the best dancer, but she didn't mind since she wasn't so great herself. Her only practice had been with friends and dancing in front of the mirror.

Peering over Eddie's shoulder afforded her a view of everyone on the dance floor, which was dappled by the twirling mirrored ball in the center of the ceiling. The walls were draped with dark blue crepe paper with silver foil stars pinned on it. Standing against a backdrop of stars in a silvery white dress was Debbie Foster, with Brandon by her side.

Tina's spirits plunged at the sight of Brandon laughing with Debbie. He was handsomely dressed in a maroon jacket and dark slacks, his hair slicked neatly into place. *I wish that was me he was talking to, not Debbie. . . .*

Then Brandon leaned over and said something into Debbie's ear, and they strolled onto the dance floor. It was a slow dance, and he took her in his arms. Tina shut her eyes and imagined herself dancing with Brandon, his hands guiding her, gazing into her eyes, and his kiss. . . .

"Tina, the dance is over." Eddie's voice cut into her dream.

Tina blinked at him. She hadn't even heard the music stop! Her cheeks flooded with embarrassment. "Oh, I was just thinking . . . I guess the music kept going in my head," she explained, knowing it was a dumb excuse.

"You're crazy." He chuckled and squeezed her hand.

The music started once more, and this time Tina forced her mind to stay on her partner. Besides, it only made her miserable to glance across the auditorium and see Debbie and Brandon together because it was obvious how much fun they were having.

After several dances, Mr. Redland climbed onstage. "You all put your names into a hat when you walked in the door, remember? Now first the girls will pick one name from this hat, and that person will be your partner for the next dance!"

Tina filed up to the stage with everyone else and picked her name.

"Who'd you get?" Eddie asked, leaning over her shoulder.

"Brandon Wells," Tina returned in a schocked near-whisper.

Numbly, she glided over to where Brandon was standing alone. When he saw her, his eyes lit up. "Hey, if it isn't the star of the six o'clock news!"

"Howdy, partner." She grinned up at him.

"*You're* my partner?" he asked.

"Yes," she replied. "Care to dance?"

"Sure." He took her in his arms, and she felt all trembly and loose as they danced across the floor. Did he realize he was part of a dream come true? Tina wondered, drinking in his intoxicating closeness, which she vowed to treasure in her memory forever.

"I hope it's OK to tell you, you look sensational, Davis," he whispered in her ear, thrilling her all the way to her toes.

"Why wouldn't it be OK?" Tina asked, thinking, I can't stop how I feel. I may never be the same again!

"I don't know. . . . You're always so prickly."

Me, prickly? Perhaps I *am* being overly sensitive, Tina considered. She didn't feel that way now, in Brandon's arms. In fact, the intensity of her feelings frightened and excited her at the same time. Brandon spun her around, his eyes never leaving hers. Time seemed suspended, and Tina was willingly pulled under Brandon's spell. Could it be like this for him, too? she wondered briefly, gazing into his face.

All too soon, the music ended, and the lights came on, breaking the spell.

"Thanks, Davis. We make a good team." Brandon grinned, and Tina thought he was about to ask her something, when Debbie claimed him, slipping her arm through his.

"Brandon, that's who you were with. Hi, Tina. I was with Tom Frankweiler—what a funny guy!" Debbie giggled.

Tina smiled, secretly wishing Debbie would disappear and leave her alone with Brandon. "See you later," she told him and took off to find Eddie.

She noticed Dallas sitting by himself and went over to join him. "Where's Marcy?" she asked.

He looked really down. "She left a little while ago. We had a fight. I think she called her mom. Like to dance?"

Dancing with Dallas was like dancing with the side of a barn, Tina thought. He was a big guy, but even big guys get broken hearts, she reflected sadly, averting her gaze from his hangdog expression.

After the dance, Eddie and Tina bought cocoa and strolled along the riverbank, holding hands.

"Do you like to write letters, Eddie?" Tina asked.

He turned to her, his puzzled expression illuminated by a full moon that spilled a wide path of gold onto the water. "No, I can't stand writing letters. I'd rather use the phone. Why?"

"Oh, just curious," she replied. *Scratch that one.* Come to think of it, Eddie never did seem like the type, anyway.

"I had a good time tonight," Eddie said.

"Me, too, Eddie. Thanks," Tina told him, and she meant it. After all, it had been a good dance, except for two things: seeing Brandon with Debbie and the trouble between Marcy and Dallas.

That one special dance with Brandon had given Tina a preview of what falling in love could be like. But on the other hand, she reminded herself, what was one dance weighed against a whole evening he spent in Debbie's arms?

Chapter Fifteen

"Dallas gave me the third degree about Aaron, and I just got so upset I had to leave." Marcy burst into fresh tears, burying her face in her pillow.

"Look, Marce, don't cry." Tina folded her arm around her friend's quaking shoulders. "I'm sorry you had such an awful time. But you've got to be straight with Dallas. He cares so much about you."

Barb shook her head at the sight of Marcy's formal crumpled into a lump on the carpet where she had dropped it the night before. Carefully she picked it up, smoothed its wrinkles, and hung it in the closet. "The guy's crazy about you, Marce," she said. "I wish somebody'd get crazy about me."

"You wouldn't wish that if you liked two boys at the same time. I mean, how do you choose?"

"You have to choose, Marcy. If you were just dating, like I'm dating Rick and Eddie. . . ."

"What about Kevin?" Barb waggled her ears and eyebrows. "The little twerp phoned me to find out who you went to the dance with!"

"No kidding?" Tina didn't remember seeing him at the dance, and she had looked at every boy as a potential letter writer, too. But Kevin remained a likely suspect. "I still say you two would make a cute couple, even with your new hair color." Tina jabbed Barb playfully in the ribs.

"Ha ha. Let's get off this subject. . . . How about Marcy's problem?"

Unfortunately, no amount of clowning could make Marcy crack a smile this morning. "Obviously, Dallas doesn't want to share you with another boy. You've got to follow your heart. Do what feels right and tell Dallas what your decision is," Tina advised.

A sob snagged in Marcy's throat as she stared, round-eyed, at her friend. "Follow my heart? Is that what you said?"

"Well—yeah." Tina began to feel uncomfortable. There was a ring of familiarity about this whole scene. "What's wrong?" she asked defensively.

"That's exactly what 'Dear Amanda' told me!"

"No kidding?" breathed Barb.

Tina gulped, seeing everything very clearly for the first time. Of course, Marcy had written that letter to Amanda, only Tina didn't know at the time she had a friend with this problem. OK, Amanda, get me out of this one. . . .

"Well, uh, then I'm glad to know I'm on the right track," Tina said, managing a small smile. What a close call—she'd have to be more careful in the future.

"There's a phone call for you." Emily held her palm over the receiver as Tina walked in the kitchen door. "Someone wants to interview you."

"Really?" Tina took the phone, half-imagining her photo on the features page of the Sunday *Herald*.

"Is this *the* Tina Davis of Channel Eight renown?"

Tina's skin rippled deliciously at the sound of Brandon's voice, but she decided to play along. "Yes, this is she," she returned coolly.

"Hi. This is Brandon Wells of the *Eagle*, and I was wondering if you'd grant me an interview."

"Oh, sure." She giggled. "What is it you want to know?"

"Well, I'd rather talk to you in person, if it's all right. Can I come over?"

Tina couldn't believe it. Brandon—at her house! "Of course," she told him eagerly, perhaps too eagerly, but it was a little late to worry about that now.

"I'll be right there," he said, then hung up.

In the minutes before Brandon arrived, Tina straightened the patio furniture, combed her hair, and put on a nice T-shirt. Memories of the dance paraded through her head, making her dizzy and anxious to see Brandon again. Naturally, today wouldn't be like last night, she cautioned herself. Last night was a dance; there had been a special atmosphere. And Brandon didn't even know how she felt about him.

But when the doorbell rang, Tina nearly jumped out of her skin. "I'll get it," she called to Emily.

"So this is where Tina Davis lives." Brandon flashed her an engaging smile.

Tina looked past him to his car parked in

front. "You didn't bring the camera crew with you, I see."

He laughed. "Not this time, Davis. It's just me, I'm afraid. Ms. Clark figured we could use your class picture and save film."

"You're funny." She led him out to the patio.

"Hey, this is great. I love it—with the brick and everything."

"My dad and I put them in," she explained, proud to have something else to her credit besides her face on TV.

"Want something to eat or drink? We've got sweet rolls."

"Sure. I never stop eating."

"Seems I noticed that about you once before." Tina got some cheese Danish and a few honey rolls from the kitchen.

"What are you going to write about me? I'm not that interesting, other than my smashing Channel Eight appearance."

He tapped his pencil against his teeth. Today his hair was all rumpled, as if he had just tumbled out of bed. "I can write about anybody and make them sound fascinating."

"Great, thanks, Brandon."

"Hey, come on. Let's start with what you're involved in at school." He chewed on a cheese

Danish as she listed a few of her favorite subjects.

"Fascinating," he said, after she had finished.

"You asked." Tina giggled.

"How many people in your family?"

She told him about Emily and her dad and the twins. "You're lucky the twins aren't here right now. They're a two-kid demolition crew," she explained.

"Can't be any worse than my brothers and sisters. There are six of us kids living in an old Victorian. Everybody says the house is haunted. It's haunted all right—by us!"

Tina laughed, imagining the warm, rough-and-tumble family Brandon came from.

"What are your goals, besides becoming a TV newscaster?"

"You're putting words in my mouth. That isn't one of my goals, as far as I know." Her eyes locked with his for one melting instant; then she looked away. Did he think about her after the dance at all, she wondered, or was his mind filled with Debbie?

"OK. How about becoming editor of the *Eagle*?"

Tina gasped. "I never thought of that, but now that you mention it . . ."

"It makes good copy, anyway," he said, scribbling it down in a small green notebook.

"I got on the newspaper staff because I wanted to get involved in school, and I always liked to write," Tina explained. "I don't know if I want to make a career of it, but I really enjoy it."

Brandon closed his notebook. "Yeah, that's me, too. Seems like you've changed this year."

"How?"

He shrugged. "I can't put my finger on it. You're just—different."

Tina's spirits soared; a bubble of laughter rose into her throat. He *did* notice her; it wasn't her imagination.

"Do you have some little bit of advice to hand out? You know, like they always have in those *People* articles?"

"Oh, come on, Brandon! I don't have any advice!" Suddenly Tina realized how funny that sounded coming from her. But then he wasn't aware that he was talking to someone with a double identity. "You can't give the same advice to everybody, anyway."

"I don't know about that. Some advice is pretty universal, like 'Neither a borrower, nor a lender be,' or 'A stitch in time saves nine.' "

"I've got one! 'Everything is funny as long as it's happening to somebody else.' "

"Hey, that's good. You know, the student council is having a meeting next week to seriously consider your safety idea." Brandon leaned back in his chair.

"Really? I suggested that on the spur of the moment. I mean, it just came to me in a burst of inspiration," she said, giggling.

"Pretty quick thinking." He shook his head in disbelief. "Did you have a good time last night?"

"Yes, did you?" Tina felt suddenly breathless. A cloud scudded across the sun, leaving Brandon's face partly shadowed.

"Sure, *Debbie* and I had a great time," he said, smiling wryly and squinting his eyes as if to gauge her reaction better.

Tina stiffened at the mention of Debbie, but she pretended not to care. "Another sweet roll?" she asked, her hand trembling as she held out the plate to him.

"No, thanks." Brandon rose to leave. "I'd better get home and type up this prize-winning interview for tomorrow."

Tina laughed nervously and walked him to the door.

"See you at school," he said, climbing into his yellow Pinto.

"See you." She waved, thinking how those words were a substitute for all that she wanted to tell him but surely never would.

Chapter Sixteen

Tina waited at Rick's locker Monday morning until he arrived. He scowled at her.

"What do you want?"

"I want to talk to you, Rick."

"What about?" He spoke curtly, not looking at her.

"I haven't seen you much lately." She stalled. How do you get to the point, when you can't say, hey, did you write a letter to "Dear Amanda"?

"So? You've been too busy with Eddie Marshall, from what I can see," he muttered bitterly, wedging books into the crook of his arm.

"That's not it," Tina said quickly. "Let me explain."

"Don't bother, Tina." His face was beet red. "I like you a lot, but I'm not going to sit around dying of a broken heart because you're dating someone else."

"I never expected you to, because it's not as if we're going together or anything like that."

Rick slammed his locker shut. "See you later. I'm going to be late for class." He spun around and sprinted down the hallway, as if he couldn't get away fast enough.

It was too bad she couldn't just say what was on her mind, instead of having to beat around the bush. But Rick was still a strong possibility—he had the attitude of someone who would write letters to "Dear Amanda."

At lunchtime, Tina went to see Ms. Clark, to pick up the "Dear Amanda" letters. Ms. Clark handed her a stack of mail. "You're really getting popular," she said teasingly.

Tina dropped the letters into her book bag. "You wouldn't happen to know anything about a 'Mystery Boy' who writes to me, would you?"

"How should *I* know?"

"Well, I'm just trying to figure out who he is. I think someone might be playing a trick on me."

"You'd better get handwriting samples from your suspects," Ms. Clark suggested. "The only person I know who's written to you is myself. I was the Green-Eyed Monster's Girl."

"My first letter!" Tina cried. "How'd it turn out?"

"We broke up." Ms. Clark smiled demurely. "He couldn't take your advice, I'm afraid."

"I'm sorry."

"Don't be. You were right, *Amanda*." She patted Tina's hand. "We can't live by other people's measuring sticks."

Ms. Clark had given Tina an idea. Although she was afraid to approach Rick again, maybe she could learn who MB was through a process of elimination.

When she got home, she found the sequined purse which had a dance card that Eddie had filled out for the fun of it. Tina was pretty sure Eddie wasn't the one, and when she compared the card to one of MB's letters, Eddie's handwriting confirmed it.

She went through her Amanda mail, checking for more letters from MB, but there were none, only the following:

Dear Amanda,

If it weren't for your column, I'd go crazy lying here with mono. Keep up the good work!

Bored Stiff

Dear Bored,

If it weren't for wonderful letters like yours, I'd go crazy writing this column! Get well soon!

Amanda

Dear Amanda,

I'm the girl who was once miserable and brokenhearted, but now I'm dating and having a great time. It was painful at first, but I'm doing OK now. Thank you for the advice. It works!

Once Miserable

Yes, I know it works, Tina thought, because I'm living it right now . . . except now that I know Brandon, dating and having fun just doesn't seem like enough. . . .

She was still worried about Marcy, who was with Dallas a lot, but they were always arguing, always on the verge of breaking up. She added:

Confidential to Double-Trouble—Let me know how you're doing. Your heart is sure to lead you to an answer soon.

Amanda

In school the next day, Tina ran into Kevin. "Oh, Kevin, you're just the person I wanted to see."

He stared at her in amazement. "I am?"

"Yes. Do you like to write, by any chance?"

"Write? You mean, like school assignments and stuff?"

"Well, uh, more like letters." Glancing at the overhead clock, Tina could see she didn't have much time. She ripped a piece of paper out of her notebook. "Here, write your name on this, would you, for me? I'm doing . . . a kind of study."

"Oh, yeah?" He scribbled his name. "I hope you're not doing a handwriting analysis. That's not my very best handwriting."

"It's just fine, Kev. Thanks, you're fantastic." She had just enough time to scoot into her next class as the bell rang.

As soon as she got the chance, Tina pulled out MB's letter to compare handwriting. Kevin wasn't the one. His handwriting was all scrunched up, whereas MB's had an easy, flowing style. The more she thought about it, the more evidence pointed to Rick being MB.

Chapter Seventeen

The journalism class was resting from the effort of putting out the paper. Some kids were doing their homework, others were playing finger football. Tina thumbed through the *Eagle*, until she found what she was looking for—Brandon's interview, entitled "That Famous Face."

> Maybe a lot of you are wondering, who is that pretty Elton student who was on the six o'clock news after Elton's big chemical scare in the science building?
>
> She's none other than Tina Davis, a member of the *Eagle* staff and the Student

Honor Society. What's more, Tina's brilliant TV speech triggered the student council to consider forming a safety committee that would weed out potential dangers in our school.

But besides being brilliant, Tina is witty, fun, and has a great sense of humor. She loves working on the newspaper and says she might enjoy being editor of the *Eagle* someday. One of her favorite sayings is, "Everything is funny as long as it is happening to somebody else."

"Like it?" Brandon pulled up a chair and sat down beside her. "Ms. Clark approved it before it ran."

"I love it, except it doesn't sound like me," Tina protested. And I can't believe you see me this way, she thought to herself. "I feel like I'm reading about some wonderful person I don't even know."

"Sure it's you." He smiled at her, and Tina was entranced by how his green shirt made the color of his eyes stand out. "I wanted to tell you I liked your article on the science scare. It turned out really well."

"Thank you," she said, a tingle starting at

her scalp and traveling all the way to her toes.

Noting her uncertainty, he said, "I mean it." Then he reached in his back pocket and unfolded a wad of papers. "I'm interviewing the science teachers as a follow-up article."

"Great idea!"

"Yeah, well, you know chemicals and the problem of storage are pretty complicated. There's more to it than you can put into one piece."

Tina had the feeling he was teasing her. Numbly, she focused on the way Brandon casually ran his papers along the palm of one hand while he talked.

"Here, take a look." Brandon unfolded the papers, the rough draft of his article. Later, Tina wondered why it had taken her so long to notice. Perhaps she was just completely hypnotized by his presence. She was halfway through the article when she realized that Brandon's flowing handwriting was unmistakably familiar to her. Tina gazed at the paper for a minute before the knowledge began to seep in.

Brandon—could it really be him? But it is! The proof is right here in front of my face!

She leaned closer, tapping the paper with her forefinger. "Good title," she said. She lifted her face to find him laughing.

Chapter Eighteen

"I still can't believe it's you," Tina whispered across the wooden table at Adolfo's. A candle flickered between them, sending shadows dancing across Brandon's face. His mouth parted in an easy smile, and Tina felt the sudden urge to know what it would be like to kiss him.

"I'm glad you saved me from anonymity," Brandon said. "I was beginning to think you were a hopeless case."

"Well, you didn't exactly make it easy," said Tina, remembering how they had crossed swords so many times. It was a miracle they were still speaking.

"It wasn't all my fault," he returned. "You're one tough lady to tangle with."

"Still full of compliments, aren't you?" Tina was secretly pleased that he thought so.

"Depends on how you take me—with salt, or pepper." He held up both shakers. "How about spicing up our relationship a little?"

"Hey, don't!" she cried, grabbing for his wrists. He put down the shakers and took her hands in his.

"Come on, let's get serious." Brandon took Tina's hand and held it against his cheek. "Come on. Let's go for a walk." Brandon paid the bill, and they walked outside, hand in hand.

The town lights began to come on, and a stiff breeze rose from the river. All those disconnected feelings Tina had been experiencing for the past couple of months started merging into something whole, and she knew that what she felt for Brandon was real love. She'd known it that day they had spent at the fair together but couldn't bring herself to believe it, let alone admit it, then. But now, everything was perfect—especially the rough feel of his fingers entwined in hers. And when he searched her eyes, she felt a magical electricity pass between them, something far beyond words.

"I feel like I already know you better than I should," Brandon said, his arm stealing around Tina's waist. "In spite of all our differences."

"Me, too. My secret pen pal." She smiled. His lips covered hers. His kiss was long and gentle. Tina wished it could go on forever—the rough feel of his cheek against hers, the wind in their hair, their bodies warming each other.

"We have to make up for lost time," Brandon whispered into her hair. "All the times I hassled you, I really wanted to kiss you."

"Really?" she asked, between his kisses.

"Yeah—what did you think? I was just some sort of wise guy or something?" He shifted his head to one side to look at her.

"That's how you acted—like I was Ms. Know-nothing. I set out to prove you were wrong."

"To tell you the truth—I was gone on you the minute I saw you, but I just couldn't let you know that. Pride, I guess. I knew you were something special, Tina, but you seemed so together. . . ."

"Me?" she asked, unable to believe it.

"Yes, you. You were different from the other girls. The paper is important to you, and you proved you really wanted to do something exciting on it, not just flirt with all the jocks like Patti and some of the others."

"You seemed like you didn't need anybody or anything."

"Yeah, well—" Brandon grinned at her. "That was a huge front. I come off that way sometimes, and I'm sorry. My dad says it's because I've always taken responsibility to heart. He says I would take on the entire universe if I could. In my big family," he explained, "I organize the games and activities. I'm in charge while Mom and Dad work, and my brothers and sisters think I'm a big pain."

Tina laughed.

"No, really. Can you imagine, six kids all trying to be accomplished at one thing or another just to stand out? That's us. And I'm the worst—obnoxious."

"That was one of my first impressions," Tina admitted.

"What were your others?"

They began walking again, holding hands.

"That I liked you," she said, smiling.

"Whew!" He looked relieved.

"One question—what about Debbie Foster? How're things between you?" Tina couldn't let that just slide by, unsolved. She had to know.

"Just as I told you, Tina. She's only a friend. I went to the dance with her because she had just broken up with her boyfriend. He goes to college near here. She needed someone to take her out, to help her get over the blues."

She punched him playfully in the arm, and he started laughing.

"How did you find out that I'm Amanda?" she asked.

"Your typewriter told me. You have a jumping *A*, so when you turned in your letters, I compared the type with your other work."

"Very clever," Tina mused. "Looks like you have a double identity, too, MB."

He chuckled. It was like having a whole relationship sleeping beneath the one you'd known all along. Tina had thought that their fiery, funny feud would never end in anything but anger, certainly not romance. Brandon was the last person on earth she ever expected to end up with, even though, in her dreams, he was the one she always wanted. At last, she thought, she could see him for what he was: a special guy hiding his hesitation behind a mask—a lot like she was doing with Amanda.

"So what does Amanda have to say about us now?" Brandon asked.

Tina gave his question a moment's consideration. "Amanda says, 'Confidential to MB—I love you.' "

Brandon's lips brushed hers. "Mmmmm. I love you, too."

Sweet
Dreams

( ) #36 SUMMER DREAMS by Barbara Conklin (On sale March 15, 1983 • 23339-4 • $1.95)

Katy's summer looks to be the most rewarding one of her life—she'll be helping Michael, a little blind boy, get over a recent tragedy, and Steve Kaplan, the boy of her dreams, will be working with her. But as the summer draws to a close Michael is turning out to be more than she can handle—and Steve, though friendly, remains distant. When they say good-bye to Michael, will Katy and Steve be losing each other, too?

( ) THE BODY BOOK by Julie Davis (On sale March 15, 1983 • 23376-5 • $1.95)

Are you happy with the shape you're in? Chances are you'd like to lose five pounds, firm up your tummy, round out your figure, or strengthen your legs. Well, you're not alone—everyone can use some improvement, and by using THE BODY BOOK'S easy-to-follow program of exercise and nutrition, *you* can decide just how healthy and attractive you'll be.

Buy these books at your local bookstore or use this handy coupon for ordering: